PUFFIN BOOKS

A Foot in the Grave

Joan Aiken / Jan Pieńkowski

Jan Pieńkowski's pictures are as original and haunting as the stories they inspired in this rare and bewitching combination of word and image.

A *Foot in the Grave* is full of spectral characters let loose in modern settings: a school cruise in the Mediterranean, a New York apartment, a city tower block, a local council meeting, a supermarket checkout. The stories all have the power and mysterious qualities of more traditional tales – and the eerie ghosts themselves are all only too plausible. A compelling read . . . but a most uncomfortable one!

Joan Aiken was born in Rye, Sussex, in 1924, the daughter of Conrad Aiken, the American writer of New England and *Mayflower* ancestry. She has worked in a variety of capacities, including for the United Nations. She has always written a great deal, and now devotes all her time to writing.

Jan Pieńkowski was born in Warsaw, and came to England as a child in 1946. A founder director of the greetings card company, Gallery Five, he has also worked in advertising, TV graphics and theatre design. Now best known for his numerous children's books, Jan Pieńkowski has twice won the Greenaway Medal.

A Foot in the Grave

Joan Aiken
and
Jan Pieńkowski

PUFFIN BOOKS

PUFFIN BOOKS

Published by the Penguin Group
Penguin Books Ltd, 27 Wrights Lane, London W8 5TZ, England
Penguin Books USA Inc., 375 Hudson Street, New York, New York 10014, USA
Penguin Books Australia Ltd, Ringwood, Victoria, Australia
Penguin Books Canada Ltd, 10 Alcorn Avenue, Toronto, Ontario, Canada M4V 3B2
Penguin Books (NZ) Ltd, 182–190 Wauiru Road, Auckland 10, New Zealand

Penguin Books Ltd, Registered Offices: Harmondsworth, Middlesex, England

First published by Jonathan Cape Ltd 1989
Published in Puffin Books 1992
1 3 5 7 9 10 8 6 4 2

Made and printed in Hong Kong

Contents

Cold Harbour 7

Movable Eyes 27

Beezlebub's Baby 40

A Foot in the Grave 48

Light Work 57

An Ill Wind 71

Bindweed 97

Amberland 115

Cold Harbour

red Skinner, our history teacher, used to make a bit of extra cash during holidays by giving lectures aboard cruise ships. Easy money, he said it was, people on those cruises fairly soon grew bored with picturesque ports and postcards and gift shops and scenic bus rides; give them a bit of solid information about Hannibal or Napoleon or the slave trade, he said, and they're as happy as sandboys and begging for more.

Being fixed up with such an eager captive audience must have been a real treat for Mr Skinner who, undersized, hatchet-faced, sandy-haired, with a big birthmark on his forehead, made a natural target for the loutish macho figures of the Lower Fifth. Three of those were his main persecutors: Pete Dummer, "Tiny" Foligno, and Goon Gold, all three large, active, and pea-brained. I've seen poor Skinner reduced to actual tears of rage and helplessness at the end of one of their classes. So, going off on a nice well-behaved cruise ship, giving talks to enthusiastic adults with free meals, trips ashore, and his own wee cabin thrown in, must have seemed like a foretaste of heaven.

Until the day when Pete, Goon, and Tiny came aboard.

In a way it was Skinner's own fault. He had boasted so much about the cruises, Corinthian Classics, they were called, and about how he and the management were on such A1 terms they were even thinking of making him an honorary director, that finally our headmaster, Claud Knott, known of course to one and all as Granny, got bitten by the cruise bug as well, went on one of them, and decided that from then on cruises should be a Cultural Extra. He got cut-price rates from Corinthian for bulk bookings, and it was amazing how many parents managed to scrape up the money, animated, perhaps, by the thought of saying goodbye to their loved ones for a couple of weeks. Mr Foligno, Mr Dummer, and Mr Gold were among them, the parents of Tiny, Pete, and Goon.

Poor Skinner. It was a bit hard on him, I thought. I happened to see his face when those three came up the gangway – sniggering a bit, and pushing each other about, as was their habit. Macbeth can't have looked much different when he saw the three witches gibbering at him from the soft shoulder. Still – luckily for Skinner – he was not actually in charge of the cruise group from our school; he'd made it plain that giving lectures was his department and he was not to be held responsible for discipline; so the Granny, sensible for once, had deputed Clem Foss, the gym teacher, and Mrs Mainspring, the school matron, to go along with the Morningquest School contingent. Foss, big, tough, bristly, without an idea in his head, would be quite equal to Goon & Co. And he knew the Med., too, because he had fought all up Italy and picked up Italian as well as a bullet at Monte Cassino, and then fought all up France and picked up French. So he wasn't about to take any nonsense from anybody. And Mrs Mainspring, though only four foot eleven, packs a terminal voltage and is quite handsome with it. She looks like a miniature tiger-lily. Nobody tangles with *her*.

The only problem, it turned out, was that neither of them was a very good sailor. Also poor Skinner had a crush, unreciprocated, on la Mainspring, and that was a weakness of his that Pete, Tiny and Goon had homed in on, as such baboons are prone to; they may not have any grey matter but they pick up vibrations like bats.

Mind you – I never *liked* Skinner. You couldn't help pitying him when the three Goons had him raging and screaming with hysteria, but basically he was a mean little character. He never did his share of syllabus advising, or helping with school plays, or the extras that most other teachers put in regularly, grumbling about it, but decent enough and really generous with their time, considering their low pay and that they don't get any overtime for it. But not Skinner. At the end of the school day he'd be out, as fast as any twelve-year-old. Ask him a question, no matter what, if you saw him outside the school grounds and "Oh, that must wait till school hours," he'd say instantly.

I saw him, one time, pick up a five-pound note, fluttering along the pavement in the High Street, and he had it whipped into his pocket, quick, like a lizard. Not a glance up and down the street to see if some poor OAP had dropped it, no; he'd palmed it like a confidence trickster. I'd never play Find the Lady with *him*.

There's a kind of lizard called a Skink. Tiny found a picture of it in the school library, and from then on Skink was his name. Or Freddie.

Another thing I didn't like about him was the way he sneaked back bits of antiquities from foreign parts. *Illegal* bits, I mean. I know Lord Elgin did it with those marbles, but he did pay for them, we're told, and nobody thought it wrong at that time. Now, foreign governments, in the kind of countries that are ninety per cent ancient ruins, take a lot of trouble to make sure that tourists don't sneak over the border wearing pre-Christian gold armbands up to their elbows, or with the Winged Victory of Samothrace tucked inside a golf-bag.

Skink, though, was quite equal to those precautions, and sniggered about it. He'd brought home a lot of little bits of statuary sunk inside pots of Greek honey; and some coins that he'd tucked into the soles of his built-up platform shoes; and a small Etruscan pot, pinched from a dig, that he'd calmly carried out stuffed inside the outer casing of a vacuum flask; and some medieval manuscript that he'd worn under his thermal vest. There were other things, too, that he hinted about but didn't show or mention. Collecting those little fragments and relics of history was his mania. Which was why – I suppose – you had to admit that he was a good teacher, really interested in what he taught, and knew a whole lot about it.

You couldn't respect him, though. I mean: if the staff don't keep to the rules, why should they expect the kids to? Old Skink was a number one rule-breaker; "Rules are for fools," he used to say scornfully. "Rules are for the mob. Because unless you have the mob all doing the same thing, there will be chaos. But of course no intelligent person need be bound by rules; they weren't meant for *him*."

On the SS *Hermes* I often saw him nip through a door labelled *Crew Only* which, he'd found, led to a quick way to the upper deck; and he had various fiddles with the black market in foreign currency, and sat all the time on the Perseus deck, which was meant to be reserved for top-class passengers. They were too polite to throw him out, I suppose. And there he was safe from Pete, Goon, and Tiny.

We embarked in Venice, in a snow-storm. Have you ever been in Venice in winter? It's the coldest town in the world. We were taken out to look at the town but, as we none of us had much money to spend, were thankful to get back on board and listen to Skink telling us about the various forms of torture used by the Doges on political prisoners. Sailing out of harbour, we passed a cortège of funeral barges, festooned with great wreaths of flowers, all covered in snow; and Skink told us that when Venetian citizens are buried on the cemetery island of San Michele their bodies are only allowed to remain there for twelve years, as the place is already overpopulated; after that the bones have to be cremated, or taken away and reburied somewhere else. If the relatives can't be contacted, the cemetery authorities make their own arrangements.

"They probably dump them in the garbage scow," sniggered Pete. He and his mates were quite interested, for once, in what Skink had to say.

I thought how angry the ghost of the dead person would be to find its remains treated in this disrespectful way; to be turned out of its resting-place.

By and large, Pete, Goon and Tiny weren't too bad for the first few days, mainly because they simply hadn't time to misbehave. While we weren't listening to lectures from Skink about the Fall of Byzantium and Hannibal's road haulage system, Foss kept us busy with yoga classes and kung-fu and swimming in the ship's pool. During the night, the *Hermes* hurtled at top speed through the Mediterranean; if you lay awake you could hear the water surging past. But we were mostly too dog-tired to lie awake. Next morning the ship would have docked at a new port, and we'd all bundle ashore, at eight-fifteen, right after breakfast, to visit the local museum, full of pots and statuary, the local ruined Greek temple and amphitheatre – the Greeks went everywhere the Americans go now – the local cathedral, castle, volcano, or grotto. Then back to the ship for lunch.

Then off in a bus to visit more distant ruins and a lecture on site about the classic Greek construction industry and government regulations. Did you know they were quite as strict and stuffy in their town planning as any set of Russian commissars? Every temple, from Asia Minor to Marseilles, had to be exactly the same size and shape as every other temple, built to pattern, just like a batch of council houses. This annoyed Skink dreadfully. He went on a whole lot about the need of freedom for artists and how this was why Greek civilisation collapsed.

The first week of the trip we visited a whole bunch of Greek islands. And one of them had a fish-market near the dock which was still operating as we came back for lunch; Tiny nipped off to it and joined us again, giggling, as we climbed up the gangway and hung up our landing-tags on the board. Everybody had a number, and you carried this little plastic square on shore with you. That way, they could be sure of not leaving any passenger on land by mistake. Skinner's, easy to remember, was 100; Tiny noted that his tag was not on the board and went snickering off with his pals to the steward's desk where they asked for Skinner's cabin key as, said Goon virtuously, "We've written essays on the Greek slavery system we want to leave for him to read." The chief steward, thinking no harm, let them have the key; and that night people on Ganymede deck were woken by fright-ful screams, as Skinner, hopping into his bunk, a bit muzzy from ouzo, found it all stuffed with live cala-mari, those little squiggly octopods that the Greeks serve with drinks before meals. Only of course those ones are fried with breadcrumbs.

Pete, Goon, and Tiny were debarred from next day's excursion, and had to spend the day on board, doing press-ups with Clem Foss. They were sore about that, because it was Santorini, where there is an active volcano and a funicular that hoists you up to the town, which is 800 feet above the harbour. And no chance of sneaking ashore on the quiet, either, for Santorini harbour, being the crater of an old volcano, is 1,400 feet deep, so the ship could not anchor, but just chugged round and round the bay all afternoon.

So that did nothing to improve relations between Skink and the three.

They spent some time writing a note to him from Juliet Mainspring. Among Tiny's gifts is one for forgery; he'll probably end up a millionaire.

"I've something important I want to tell you; meet me on the Perseus deck at ten-thirty tonight," it said. They poked it under his cabin door. And then watched giggling from a shadowy point of vantage on the Jason deck as he waited and waited and waited, wearing his best linen jacket and a silk cravat. Finally he gave it up and went down to the lounge, the three following. They saw him go up to the Mainspring, sitting with the cruise director, and speak to her; saw her shake her head; then he turned and saw the three, falling about with laughing, and an awful look came over his face.

I did feel sorry for him then.

Things were quiet as we steamed across to Sicily and up the Tyrrhenian Sea. The three bided their time, waiting for opportunity or inspiration. We inspected plenty more ruins. People began to grumble that, since all the places we visited had been totally smashed for about twenty-six centuries, nobody had a chance to do any shopping and pick up souvenirs – except, of course, the kind that Skink snatched from archaeological sites when no one was looking.

So Jasper Tarn, the cruise director, kindly promised us that we would be given one proper shopping day, just before we made our final landfall at Nice; we would anchor at a nice picturesque little Italian fishing port where there was no history to speak of but lots of shops, stalls, and boutiques; "enough to supply next year's Christmas gifts for all your parents, aunts, uncles, brothers, sisters, and grandparents," he assured us.

Sure enough, Portofreddo, when we anchored in its harbour, was all set about, up and down, in a deep little cove, full of olives and pine trees, and was cute as any Cornish village.

I heard somebody ask Skinner if there were really no historical facts connected with it at all? And he said, well, he'd never visited it, but he'd certainly never heard of any. It had three churches, worth a visit, no doubt, one of them with an unusual graveyard; and there was a legend connected with the place, something about the spirits of people who die there, but he knew no more than that.

"Portofreddo," sniggered Pete as we went down the gangway. "That's where Freddo Skinner's going to get his comeuppance."

"Freddo means cold," said Tiny, who had Italian grandparents.

Portofreddo, I thought. That would be the same as Coldharbour in English. Oddly enough, the place did seem cold as we went ashore, perhaps because it was sunk so deep in its crevice in the cliffs. A decided chill came over us as we stepped ashore, which decided me not to stay in the port but to take a path up the wooded cliff. I'd brought my binoculars with me.

The little town was pretty as a postcard. The streets were paved with pebbles in patterns, the balconies were smothered with red and pink blossoms, the harbour was packed with fancy yachts, large and small. And the prices in most of the shops were strictly for millionaires.

I saw a sign "To the lighthouse" pointing towards the tree-covered promontory; so I followed the direction of its pointing arm. As I did so, I noticed Skink, on a parallel, lower path which went to one of the three churches, that of Santa Lucia, with the uncommon graveyard.

And I noticed Tiny, Pete, and Goon following him at a careful distance.

My path went in zigzags up the hillside, first among ritzy little houses, then among trees. Looking down, from a higher elbow of the track, I saw our good ship *Hermes* moored in the middle of the harbour. I also found that I was looking straight down, from above, into the graveyard of Santa Lucia. And it certainly was the queerest cemetery I'd ever seen. It was like a large, square room, cut out from the steep hillside, with an entrance at the rear of the church, which was built on a shelf of hill. The floor of the little cemetery was paved with graves – every inch of it, every centimetre. There must have been a couple of hundred, packed close together. Marble slabs, marked in black and white squares, like chessboards. Perhaps the ghosts come up at night, I thought, and play chess. There were dozens of statues of saints all over the end of the church; enough to act as chessmen. Then, as well, the sides of the graveyard-room were also used as tombs; the walls were completely occupied with marble cupboard doors. They had hinges. Some of them were incised with little niches, which held lighted lamps, and jars of flowers, silver-framed photos, scrolls inside glass cases, pot-plants, kids' toys, badges, medals, bits of lace and embroidery, every possible kind of reminder of the dead person. One or two of them had rugs or shawls draped over – perhaps to keep the body warm? To keep out the draughts? It was really spooky. All those marble cupboards, and up above them the granite rock. And if there were all those things outside, what might there be inside? Besides the bones, I mean? I spent about fifteen minutes staring at the place through my binoculars, taking it all in. I'd never seen anything like it.

Presently, along comes Skink, finished evidently with his inspection of the church. First he stands quite still and stares all round him; then begins prowling about. He'd said before that he'd never been to Porto-freddo – it wasn't a place Corinthian Cruises regularly visited, because of its lack of history. But I could see that Skinner was fascinated by the graveyard, just like me, and he began peering at the cupboard doors, studying their inscriptions and offerings. Next, he got to trying one or two, to see if they opened.

Oh-oh, I thought.

Most of them didn't, but a few did – they'd have keys in the locks and he'd turn them and peer inside. Generally he shut them up again pretty quick. But when he opened one – a big one, newish – he seemed to get quite excited.

He glanced about him, sharp and wary – then pulled something quite heavy and bulky out of the tomb-cupboard. A bit of folded material, brownish-reddish-purple, it was. He unfolded it, and what he saw seemed to excite him even more.

He gave another cagey look all round – he never thought to look *up* – then whipped off his windcheater jacket and wrapped this piece of stuff all round him, doubled, like a towel, tucking it inside his jeans. Then he swiftly put his jacket back on and zipped it up the front. Then, looking very nonchalant and carefree indeed, he started strolling back in the direction of the port.

I felt a bit sick. Pinching things from historical ruins was one thing – I suppose you *can* say, in a way, that history belongs to everybody – but nicking things from *graves* seemed something else. What would the dead person have to say? Supposing they knew about it? Or their family, if they were still alive?

Very bothered, I put my field-glasses back in their

case, and walked on to the point where the lighthouse was. But I didn't enjoy the walk. I was too churned up inside, wondering whether I ought to tell somebody about what Skinner had done; or not. Tell *who*? The cruise director? the ship's captain? or tackle Skinner himself? Doing any of those things seemed to make me into a sneak or a prig, and yet I honestly couldn't feel that he should be allowed to get away with it.

By and by I walked back, taking a different path, lower down the cliff, which brought me along by the church and graveyard. But I didn't linger there; I was too disturbed, and also it was far too cold. The sun had dropped behind the headland by now, the place was in deep shadow, and there was a mortal chill everywhere; the place felt as glacial as the Polar circle – an icy, damp, bone-gripping cold. So, ignoring the lamplit stalls along the quayside, with their pottery, and semi-precious stones, and handwoven fol de rols, and all the fancywork that people make in every country specially for tourists to buy, I scurried up the gangway. Putting my tag back on the board I saw that Skink's was still missing; so were those – 27, 28, and 29 – of Pete, Goon, and Tiny. For the first time I remembered them. Hadn't they been planning to play another of their tricks on Skinner? As I thought this, I saw them all coming across the quay – Skinner ahead, walking very casually, his hands in his pockets, and, a few yards behind, in a bunch, the three musketeers, jostling one another, grinning, watching Skink out of the corners of their eyes.

The dinner gong had just gone, and most people were already in the dining saloon – except for those who had chosen to stay ashore and buy themselves terribly expensive pizzas. The landing lobby was empty. But just at this moment Mrs Mainspring came down the stairs into it, with Jasper Tarn, the cruise director. He was a big bearded man who looked like Zeus and got treated like Zeus by everybody, passengers and crew alike. Whatever he said, went.

Skink stopped by Jasper Tarn to say something, smiling, a bit smarmy, and, as he did so, Pete and Goon edged up close behind him. Then Pete cried out, "Oh, sir! There's a great big hornet, or something, flew right under your jacket. Watch it! It'll sting you, it'll sting you, sir!"

Next thing, neat as a pickpocket, Goon unzipped the jacket and Pete whipped it off from behind. And there was Skinner, revealed, for all to see, wrapped in what looked to me like some kind of Persian rug. (Afterwards Mrs Mainspring told me that it was a very old one, probably worth thousands.)

Then, of course, the fat was in the fire.

Pete, Goon, and Tiny, incandescent with virtue, told how they had seen Skinner swipe the rug from the tomb. They must have been perched somewhere among the trees below me.

Skinner just stood there, white and sick-looking. He tried, just once, to make a joke of it, but Tarn wasn't having any of *that*.

"This finishes your connection with Corinthian Cruises, Skinner," he said, cold as doom. And Mrs Mainspring cried out, "Oh, Fred, how could you, how *could* you?" for although she didn't much like Skinner she was a bit sorry for him, I think, maybe used to feel he got a bit of a raw deal. Being so undersized and puny.

"You are extremely lucky that I don't instantly inform the Italian police," says Jasper Tarn. "And I shall, unless you restore the rug, right away, to the gr– er, the place from which you stole it."

"Should we go with him, sir – to make sure he does?" suggested Pete, all eager and slimy.

"No. That will not be necessary," said Tarn, giving a long hard look at Skink, who, like a thrashed dog, turned round, took his number tag off the board again, and stumbled back down the gangway.

Tarn and Mrs Mainspring, after talking together a bit in low voices, walked into the dining-room. They looked gloomy and depressed. I went after them, feeling a bit sorry for Skinner. Not very, but a bit. Also I suspected that Goon & Co. were about to play yet another of their tricks on him, probably some kind of spooky one in the graveyard.

I had seen two of them (Tiny, for reasons best known to himself, had apparently chosen to stay behind) take off after him down the gangway, grinning and nudging each other.

I felt worried about Fred. I thought he'd had about as much as he could take for one day.

The *Hermes* was scheduled to sail at 11 p.m. and all landing tags were supposed to be back on the board by 10. When it was found, at 10.05, that three were missing, there was a rare old to-do and uproar; the ship was scoured from stem to stern, so as to make sure that they were not asleep in their cabins or anywhere else (which they were not of course); announcements kept blasting out over the Tannoy, and search parties were sent ashore.

Knowing that Skinner had been bound for the graveyard of Santa Lucia, the first party went there directly. And that was where they found the two boys, crouched, clinging to each other, bawling like three-year-olds, witless with fright, and, for several hours, incapable of telling a rational story.

And when they had recovered, they weren't much more informative.

"The hole. He fell through the hole," they kept saying.

"Hole? What hole? There's no hole in the graveyard."

But the priest and *carabiniere*, who had been fetched, crossed themselves, and one of them said something about "la larva." What a *larva* was, nobody explained.

At last, quieting somewhat after they had been given a bunch of tranquillisers, the two said that when Skink approached the cupboard grave and opened its door (they, as before, had been watching from higher up the hill, planning to drop a wet rag on his head) they heard a tremendously loud creaking sound – "like ships' timbers creaking, it was," shivered Pete – and, as soon as the grave door was shut and locked, the marble slab under Skink's feet simply opened, and he fell through.

"Like a trapdoor," said Goon.

"He let out an awful, awful howl," said Pete.

"Something went down *with* him."

"He was fighting it off."

"That must have been the thing I saw," muttered Tiny, who, very pale, had been listening to his friends' account.

"What *thing*? What did you see?" demanded Jasper Tarn.

"It was like a bag of bones, wrapped up in fish skin," mumbled Tiny, who looked just about ready to throw up. "I saw it follow all the way behind him, the first time, from the graveyard to the ship. It didn't go on board. It was waiting for him, down on the dock, I expect." He began to cry. "It *stank*, too – worse than codliver oil."

"You boys must go to bed – *at* once," said Mrs Mainspring.

*

Fred Skinner was never seen again. Nor was his landing tag.

Pete and Goon don't go about with Tiny any more. They say he should have told them about the thing he saw. Suppose it had got *them*?

Movable Eyes

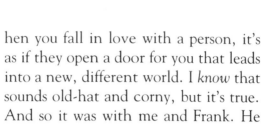

hen you fall in love with a person, it's as if they open a door for you that leads into a new, different world. I *know* that sounds old-hat and corny, but it's true. And so it was with me and Frank. He brought me into the world of Art, about which, before that time, I had known nothing at all. Now I can look at a picture and say, "That is by Courbet. That's a Picasso. That's a Hockney," and get some good out of them. Which is just as well, for there isn't much other good in my story.

I first met Frank when I had borrowed an apartment in New York (I help run a messenger service and we were starting up a branch there). One evening I heard a bang on the door.

"Who is it?" I called cautiously through the peep-hole, and was not at all reassured by the deep-voiced answer which came back:

"The Exterminator."

However I soon discovered that it wasn't me the man had come to exterminate, but simply the cockroaches with which the place was infested, so I gladly let him in. He was a big, black-bearded fellow, very gentle really, not in the least like an Exterminator, and we got friendly, and he took me to art galleries, which are, luckily, free, for he had very little money. The reason for this was that he could spare time only for a part-time job, as most of his day was spent in looking after his old mum, who was bedridden. She was in her eighties; so, precious little chance of her ever getting up out of that bed.

Frank took me home to see her, because fairly soon she began to ask querulously why he wasn't coming straight back from his exterminating round.

"Besides, she'll be glad of new company," he said. "She loves to see people."

So we went to their apartment, which was on the twenty-second floor of a big city block.

Frank's mother was a bit of a shock, I won't deny.

"Call me Zia Tisna, my sveetheart," she said. "All Franco's friends call me Zia Tisna."

Zia Tisna had come from Sicily about seventy-three years ago. She was as thin as a wisp, with a completely bloodless bony face, thin grey hair done up in a knot, and pale grey eyes hugely magnified behind lenses thick as pancakes. She wore a brilliant red dress, covered by a hand-crocheted shawl. Her long pointed

fingernails and her lips were painted the same brilliant red. She smoked non-stop – small black cigarettes in a stained ivory holder. She spoke very slowly, in a soft high quavery voice.

"So you are Eenglish?" she said, stroking my face delicately with one razor-sharp clawlike nail. "The Eenglish are all very good – no? You vill not take my son Francisco away from me? He is all I have."

And she cast Frank a wan, wistful look. His personality seemed to have altered completely as soon as he stepped inside the door. From being a large, good-looking friendly character with a Master's degree in art history, he had become a weak, hesitant lumpish type, much too big and clumsy for the room he was in.

When Zia Tisna told me that Frank was all she had, I could not help silently disagreeing with her.

For she also had the dolls. Or, as she called them, "the Creatures".

Zia Tisna made dolls. She must have been making them for the last thirty years. They were quite large; most of them over two feet high. They were made, she told me with quavery pride, from anything she could lay hands on: old coffee tins, fruit-juice jars, broken umbrellas – anything. These basic foundations were covered with materials that she had found discarded in rubbish bins all around the neighbourhood, which was full of small garment factories. Now Franco found them for her. The materials were dazzlingly gaudy – spots, stripes, brilliant colours, wrapped and draped and tucked and rucked and stitched and folded and swathed. On top of these intensely bright fabrics she had sewed spangles, beads, cheap imitation jewellery, buttons, bits of tinsel, paste, tassels, artificial flowers, sequins, feathers – all the bright and shining items that she could come by. The effect was indescribable. *One* of those creatures would have been startling enough, but the room, indeed the whole apartment, was *lined* with them. There were three quite large rooms, all full of dolls, and the effect was like stepping into an Oriental temple packed with images of nameless gods. Or a sea grotto where the walls are covered in coral and sea-anemones.

"Do you like zem?" quavered Zia Tisna in her wistful shaky voice.

What could I say? I could hardly tell her that I thought them the most eerie, sinister, grotesque objects I had ever laid eyes on, that they gave me the cold grue, just to look at them.

I said, truly, that they were remarkable, amazing, unique, that I had never seen anything like them.

"Zen you shall have vun for yourself. Vich vould you like? Zat vun is Greta Garbo, zat vun is Stalin, zat vun is Queen Elizabeth, zat vun Abraham Lincoln."

I could not detect much resemblance to the people she named, except that Stalin had a moustache made of black pipe-cleaners and Queen Elizabeth held a sceptre made from a bicycle pump covered with gilt paper.

In the end I chose Donald Duck. I thought I'd feel safer with one not intended to represent a human. The humans were too ghastly. If I owned one of them I'd be obliged to lock it in a cupboard. And then I would be thinking about it all the time, inside there. I would be wondering what it was doing; if it was angry at being shut in.

How Frank managed to endure living in a whole house full of them!

The first time I met Zia Tisna I thought she must be desperately ill, at death's door really, but I soon began to realise that she had been this way for a long time, years perhaps. She was well enough to lie in bed, smoke forty cigarettes a day, and continually make more dolls. Her rate of production was high; she could easily make two or three in a week.

"Couldn't you sell some of them – perhaps to a museum – a children's home?" I suggested to Frank, though it was not possible to feel they were suitable for children's toys.

But – "She won't part with them," Frank said. "Can't bear for them to go out of the place." Indeed – greatly to my relief – the handing-over of Donald Duck was indefinitely postponed. First she had to sew some more gold sequins on top of his head – a few more plumes – a little yellow satin. She never did get around to parting with him. In the meantime she had enlisted me in the quest for materials; I used to bring her in bundles of stuff, materials and tapes, ribbon, embroidery silks; she took them as her due and frequently grumbled about the quality.

"Zese are ter-rible poor ribbons; nossings are made, zese days, as zey used to be."

Her heart's desire was to acquire some movable eyes.

"Zey make zem so now for dolls, I have read in a magazine."

"But movable eyes are very expensive, Mama," said Frank.

"And I really don't think you need them," I soothed her. "Your dolls' eyes seem to follow one about as it is, they are made of such bright things."

This was true. If Frank gave me a quick secret kiss in the kitchen, I felt that all the sequins and boot-buttons were trained on us, all the bedizened, staring inhabitants were getting ready to report on us to their mistress.

With Frank, his mother was alternately bossy and whining.

"Ay, ay, Francisco mio, I *know* zat some day you vill go off and leave zis poor old Mama. So much trouble as she is to you!"

And of course he'd promise that he would never, never leave her, never entrust her to the harsh care of strangers.

"Do not ever let zem take me to the hospital, Franco mio! Zere zey vill keell me for sure!"

But, much more often, she would nag and scold, demanding all kinds of food that was hard to procure – "Rrreal Italian figs, figlio mio. And a salad viz radicchio! And a sorbet – just a leetle – leetle – pineapple sorbet. And you must make me some Vichyssoise – but it must be cold, *cold*, not hot – vell, vell, chill it, zen! – put it in ze freezer!" And all the time the soup was chilling, she would be grumbling at him, for not having made it at breakfast time, so that it would be cold, ready for her lunch.

"But, Mama, at breakfast time you said you wanted gnocchi for your lunch."

"Never! I said no such zing!"

Then she would weep and beg and implore him not to go off and abandon her to starve.

I did sometimes wonder how she would manage if he had to leave her for a couple of days. I had a shrewd suspicion that she was not quite so bedridden as she appeared to be. Traces of her cigarette ash could sometimes be found across the rug and into the bath-room or kitchen, though she swore that she could not walk a step unaided. She was a terrifyingly careless smoker, and frequently charred her sheets or set them on fire; Frank never dared leave her for too long. It amazed me that the embroidery and silks, the wools, the remnants of muslin and gauze that lay scattered over her bed did not ever go up in flames. I suppose she was more careful with them. While engaged on creating a doll, she could be silent for hours on end, stitching and contriving; she liked to have the television on then, with the sound off.

"Ze pictures keep me company," she sighed. "When Francisco leaves me alone, so many many hours togezzer."

"You'll simply have to get her into a nursing home soon," I told Frank. "You can't go on like this much longer."

He looked harassed, hunted. "I honestly believe she'd put a curse on me."

"You need a break. Badly. Look at you! You're in terrible shape. You should go to Europe for two or three weeks. France, Italy. Go to museums, galleries. Surely she could go into a home for *two weeks?*"

"I couldn't afford it. The fare to Europe *and* a residential home – "

But he looked desperately tempted. There was anguish in his voice.

"I could lend you the money, Frank. The agency here has started off well – "

"How could I possibly borrow from you?"

"Oh, *come* on – "

"She'd never approve."

What business is it of hers, the old witch, I thought; but of course I could see he'd have to account for the cash somehow.

"Well, at least put it to her," I said. "Try." The thought of strolling with Frank in Paris, in Florence, was very sweet. He blossomed so, away from his mother. He would be able to tell me so much, explain so much . . .

Of course his proposal of such a holiday to Zia Tisna brought on a fearful scene.

"*Dio mio!* To spend so much on such a selfish plan, ven you vill not even buy me ze movable eyes! *She* has turned you against your own muzzer, zat stony-hearted Eenglish beetch!"

And from that time on I was forbidden to set foot in the apartment, obliged to meet Frank for secret short half-hours snatched from his cockroach-exterminating job.

We were both miserable. My work in New York was nearly finished. The office was running well, ready to hand over to locally recruited staff. In three weeks I would fly back to England.

We'd probably never see each other again.

But I swear the final idea didn't come from me. I *swear* it.

Perhaps just a mention.

"That stuff you use to exterminate the bugs with. Is it very lethal?"

One morning Frank phoned me, his voice trembling.

"Mama had a bad seizure in the middle of the night. She fell out of bed and broke her hip. I – I had to get an ambulance, take her to the hospital. Will – will you come with me to visit her?"

He sounded scared to go alone. Why?

Of course I said I would.

In fact there was no terrible accusation – if that was what he had feared? We found her comatose, her plastered leg in a sling, all kinds of drips leading into her, and all kinds of tubes leading out.

Maybe she did slip and fall by accident, I thought in huge relief. Maybe there is nothing else the matter with her.

Indeed, the surgeon who had operated on her broken hip said that she was amazingly tough for her age. Even in her drugged sleep her hands kept moving – working away, like the paws of a sleeping cat, as if her deep dreams were concerned with putting another of the crazy manikins together.

"I suppose I ought to have brought some of them to the hospital," Frank said. "But the nurses wouldn't like them at all. How soon can she come home, doctor?" he asked. But the doctor shook his head and would make no promise.

Next day when we came to visit Zia Tisna, she was running a high temperature and was flushed and restless. The nurse said, "Ah, that's the trouble with these old ones. They may get over the fracture, but then pneumonia sets in – "

Zia Tisna suddenly opened her eyes and looked at us.

"Mama cara!" said Frank. His voice shook – with guilt, with grief? "What can – is there anything we can bring you?"

"Cigarettes!" she hissed. Frank shrugged and spread out his hands apologetically. He knew cigarettes would never be allowed.

Zia Tisna's eyes wandered to me. The glint of malice in them was indescribable.

She seemed to be gathering her strength. I waited in suspense.

After a moment, weakly, she whispered, "Bring me – bring me some movable eyes!"

And then she closed her own eyes and drifted off into slumber again.

Two days later she died, without regaining consciousness.

Frank decided that it would be proper to take her ashes back to Catania, where she was born, and have them interred there, in the family plot. Arranging this took time – you cannot transport somebody's ashes overseas without filling in a lot of forms – but at last it was accomplished. Frank gave all the old girl's dolls to the Ethnological Museum at Catania. They seemed rather astounded at the gift, but accepted the creatures with reasonable grace.

After that, Frank and I were free to indulge in our European trip. We travelled to Florence, to Pisa, Siena. We went to Urbino. In the Ducal Palace at

Urbino there is a famous portrait of a dumb lady, by Raphael. The eyes are supposed to follow you, wherever you walk. And it is true, they do. They *roll* after you.

I could not wait to get out of that room.

They were like Zia Tisna's eyes, flashing and malignant, full of awareness.

We took a plane from Pisa to Paris, we visited the Louvre galleries. And in the Louvre it was much worse. Much, much worse. Every single portrait – and there are hundreds, maybe thousands – had eyes that turned and followed me, rolling, gleaming with malice and knowledge.

In the end my nerve broke and I started to scream at Frank.

"Why do they all of them look at *me?*" I screamed. "It was you – you – you – who gave her the poison!"

And stumbling – dropping my purse – my throat blocked, my eyes blurred by tears – I rushed away and left him standing there.

Beezlebub's Baby

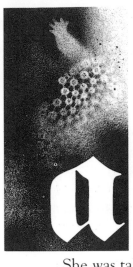

aunt Ada came to live with us at the end of the summer holidays. Before, we'd only seen her at Christmas and didn't realise just how awful she was. Now, we had her all the time.

She was tall and pale with a face like a melon and hair done in a grey knob on top of her head. Her eyes were the colour of cherrystones. Her skirts came almost to her ankles. And her voice went non-stop.

"Don't you eat that orange in here, miss! Take it in the garden. Let me see those hands, young man. *Just* as I thought. You go straight off and wash them. *What* is that *dog* doing on that *bed?*"

"Can't you stop her, Mum?" I asked, but Mum said helplessly, "She is your father's elder sister, you see . . . "

Dad, who is a merchant seaman, went to sea for longer and longer trips.

Aunt Ada had Stuart's room, and Stu had to move in with Kev. I was lucky being a girl, I had a room of my own. At least I thought I was lucky . . .

Aunt Ada took over the shopping from Mum, she said that was only fair. What wasn't fair, she expected me to help her, after I got home from school.

Which was why we were coming out of the Dick Turpin shopping mall at half-past five on a cold October afternoon, each carrying two frightfully heavy bags of shopping.

"No use waiting for a bus, love," said a man at the Swilly Valley Service stop. "They're out on strike."

"Disgraceful!" said Aunt Ada, and she carried on and on about the wicked ways of bus drivers.

"We'd better start walking," I said sadly. "It's only a mile and a half."

"We'd best go along the tow-path," said Aunt Ada. "That's only half the distance."

"Oh no, don't let's do that," I said in a great hurry.

"Why ever not?" snapped Aunt Ada, staring at me with her cherrystone eyes.

"Because – because it's sure to be muddy."

"Don't be ridiculous, child! It hasn't rained all week. Come along and don't argue. I never *met* such children for argument."

"*Please* don't let's go that way," I said again. Dusk was beginning to thicken along Potter's Road; by the time we got to the canal bridge, it would be quite dark.

"Quiet, miss! I don't want to hear another word.

Come along now – step out! Don't show me that sulky face."

And she stomped on ahead, every now and then turning round to glare at me, and make sure that I was following.

Well, I thought, she'll see it first. That's one comfort.

Another comfort was that our dog Turk wasn't with us. Turk will never, ever go along that stretch of the tow-path; he just turns round and runs home if anyone tries to take him that way, even in broad daylight.

By the time we got to the canal bridge, it was full dark. And I could hear the sound long before we got there.

So could Aunt Ada.

"That's funny," she says. "I can hear a baby crying. Can *you* hear a baby, Janet?"

"Yes," I said glumly, because I could.

"This is *no* time of day for a baby to be out," said Aunt Ada. "Its mother ought to be ashamed of herself! I've a good mind to tell her so."

I didn't think its mother would have bothered much about Aunt Ada's bad opinion even if she had heard it, two hundred years ago.

"Where can that baby be? Can it be under the bridge?" Aunt Ada said.

As we drew near, the street-lights up above shone down on the path, and made the blackness under the bridge seem even blacker. And the crying became louder and angrier.

"*I* believe," said Aunt Ada, "*I* believe that some-body's *left* that baby under the bridge. Well – that somebody is going to be in bad, bad trouble!"

And she stepped into the darkness under the bridge. I lagged back, but she called, "Come *on*, Janet!"

Still, I was far enough back so that I could see the baby, all wet and dripping, and with a faint shine about it, like a dead fish that's gone bad, come climb-ing out of the canal water and run to Aunt Ada.

She dropped both her shopping bags; oranges and yoghurt cartons and toilet rolls shot in all directions.

I had expected that Aunt Ada would run off, screaming blue murder. Most people do that, when they see a ghost baby. But not she.

"Why, you poor, poor little mite!" she said. "Who *put* you in that water? Who did such a dreadful thing?"

"It was his mother – " I began to say. "She was a highwayperson two hundred years ago – she was called Beezlebub Bess – "

But Aunt Ada was taking no notice of me. She was cosseting that baby, patting it and clucking over it like a hen that finds a diamond egg in the nesting box.

"*You*'ll have to manage the shopping the rest of the way, Janet," she says to me. "I have to carry this poor little half-drowned angel."

And she picks up the ghost baby. Angel it certainly was not.

I don't think anyone had ever picked it up before.

44

Mostly they run for their lives. A few have dropped dead on the spot. The baby wasn't at all used to being picked up. It struggled.

"None of that, now!" she said, giving it a smart shake. And to me: "Poor thing, it's as light as a feather. Half starved, I daresay. Come *on*, Janet, look sharp, pick up those bags and let's be off. The sooner this little angel is into some dry clothes the better."

"But you can't take it to our home!" I said.

"Why ever not?" She was striding away along the path as fast as her long skirts would allow. She didn't stop to listen to me.

"It's a highwaylady's baby! She dropped it in the canal when the Bow Street runners were chasing her. Her name was Beezlebub Bess!"

Aunt Ada paid no heed; so I didn't go on to tell her that Bess's black horse Jericho had jumped clean over the twenty-foot canal and so helped its mistress escape from the runners. What became of her after that was never known. But the baby which fell into the canal was drowned, and had been making a ghostly nuisance of itself ever since on the tow-path. Some people call it the Wicked Baby, and not for nothing.

"You can't take it home!" I repeated.

But Aunt Ada did.

"I *really* don't think we can have that baby in the house," said Mum helplessly.

Mum is helpless just when she ought to be firm.

45

"And what Edward will say I can't imagine," she added.

"Edward won't be home for five months," Aunt Ada said. "And the baby can sleep in Janet's room."

My room! But Aunt Ada went to the United Baptists' Jumble Sale and bought a carrycot for 50p.

At night the baby was a real menace. When it wasn't crying, grizzling, or whimpering, it would be out of the cot and fidgeting around the room. Nothing was safe. Books and tapes fell off shelves, bottles and pots rolled off the chest-of-drawers, clothes were dragged off hangers, and in the middle of the night I'd feel its tiny little ice-cold fingers scrabbling at me or pulling my hair.

How would you like to share your bedroom with a ghost baby?

Turk wouldn't come in my bedroom any more, not even into the house, he stood and growled in the back doorway.

Elsewhere in the house, the baby was just as much of a hazard. One look from it was enough to send the TV into spirals. The lights fused if it crawled across the room; and a chicken that Mum put in to roast came out frozen instead, just because little Beezlebub went and peered in the oven ten minutes before dinnertime.

The boys and I couldn't stand it any longer. We wrote to Dad. He phoned from Cairo and told Aunt Ada that she must find somewhere else to live.

To our amazement this didn't faze her at all.

"I've already thought of that," she told him calmly. "I have applied for sheltered Council accommodation, for me and my little angel. And I am pleased to say that they have put me at the top of the waiting-list."

Another month went by; but we felt we could bear it now, so long as we knew that it wouldn't be for ever. We could bear the baby's tearing up the mail in the letterbox, and eating Turk's dinner out of his bowl, turning the washing in the machine bright scarlet, making Mum's cake-mix taste as salty as the Sahara. We could bear the neighbours grumbling because it howled all night long, and the gas-meter-man refusing to call because he got his ankles bitten, and sending huge estimated bills.

We could bear the freezing cold in the house, and fish swimming in the bath.

We could bear it all if we knew the pair were going.

Well, in the end, Aunt Ada did go to her sheltered accommodation. But, guess what? The baby wouldn't stay there. She took it there okay, but it comes right back. It drifts through windows, it slides through keyholes. Night after night, there it is in my room, grizzling, scrabbling, rummaging in my drawers, poking me with its icy little fingers. The neighbours still complain, but what can we do?

It's got fond of us, see.

A Foot in the Grave

ometimes when you pull down an old house, you disturb whole troops of rats, who are obliged to move out and find another home. When you use an old graveyard as a building site, you dislodge whole troops of ghosts.

At least that's how it seemed it was going to be in the case of our great-aunt Millicent.

Great-aunt Millie was a very, very learned lady, the first woman to become Chancellor of Pen-y-Gent University. She had translated the Hebrew testament into Eskimo, and invented biplanetism, and could do any mathematical problem in her head, between two ticks of the clock. As well she was president of the Ladies' Alpine Club and captain of the Pen-y-Gent ice-hockey team. Under her scholar's gown she wore Rational Dress – that was a long blouse and baggy breeches. Also she was believed to have the Evil Eye;

people around the town and university of Pen-y-Gent were careful how they crossed her. She could turn them into mice, it was said.

Aunt Millie died in 1941 and was buried in the old Differentiated Baptist burying-ground, on the outskirts of the town, overlooking the River Swilly. As it turned out, she was the very last person to be buried there, more and more people choosing to be cremated and scattered, or interred in the big town cemetery alongside the motorway, where there was more to look at and better upkeep of the graves. In fact the Differentiated Baptist graveyard wasn't kept up at all, as the only Differentiated Baptists left in the town were by now all over eighty; and some people said the place was getting to be a disgrace, with the gravestones all toppled over, and big trees growing, and a mass of brambles everywhere so you could hardly force your way through.

Well, no one was very surprised when a firm of developers, Gussith and Inglejaw, managed to buy up the whole area, cheap, and put in for planning permission to remove the gravestones to a Garden of Remembrance (with such remaining bones as might be found), erect fifteen Homes of Distinction on half the site, and turn the other half into a cricket pitch. They would have tried for thirty Homes of Distinction, but their lawyer told them the Council would never swallow that; also Silas Inglejaw, one of the partners, was a keen cricketer and bowled for Pen-y-Gent first eleven.

There was a long piece all about this in the Pen-y-Gent *Clarion*, and our mum became very indignant.

"They've no right to do it!" she said. "Not with Aunt Millie buried there. It's not respectful."

"Blest if I see what you can do about it," grunted Grandpa, mixing away at his compost. All he ever thinks about is compost.

But Mum is not Great-aunt Millie's niece for nothing. She went to see my friend Tod's father, he teaches civics and legal history at the university. Sure enough, he found that the Disused Burial Grounds Amendment Act (passed in 1981) forbids the erection of buildings in a graveyard if there are objections from relatives of anyone buried there during the last fifty years.

So you see Great-aunt Millie came just inside that category, and therefore nothing could be done with the place until 1991.

Tod's dad wrote to Gussith and Inglejaw pointing this out, and he sent a copy of his letter to the Pen-y-Gent *Clarion* too.

Silas Inglejaw was furious, of course.

He decided that the simplest thing would be to pretend he never received Tod's father's letter, but just go ahead and start digging up the graveyard. After all, once the deed was done, it would be too late to stop him.

So he had his excavators go along one evening, about eight o' clock, and they dug up a whole row of graves, along the west side of the graveyard, from Chapel Street junction with Trader's Passage down to the bank of the River Swilly.

"Never mind the overtime expense," Inglejaw told the contractors. "Just get it done. It's worth it to me."

But he reckoned without Mum, who was keeping a sharp eye on the graveyard from our attic window. As soon as she saw the excavators go in she phoned the Clerk of the Council, Fred Owen-Moon, who plays billiards every Friday with my uncle Swithin, and Fred was round at the graveyard in ten minutes, and what he said about laying injunctions and £50,000 fines put such a fright on the contractors that they stopped their digging and rolled their excavators out of there in less time than it takes to tell.

But of course already a whole row of graves had been grubbed up, and ten tombstones piled against the wall: John Lewin, Amos Higgs, five members of the Jones family, Hezekiah Pwell, Ann Landers, Phoebe Gurney, and Mr and Mrs Davies. Besides two big trees cut down. What a mess! Earth heaved up every which way, two huge ilexes lying across the graveyard, and piles of dug-up brambles twenty feet high.

I happened to come home half an hour after that (I play board number three for Pen-y-Gent at the Junior Chess Club on Thursday nights) just at owl-light, when trees and houses are black and the sky pale-green, and all along the churchyard wall I saw this row of ghosts sitting, like old fowls gone to roost, grimy and dusty and tattered, wailing and muttering and grumbling and carrying-on, like a schoolteachers' union meeting when they can't agree about pension rates.

I went home and told Mum about it.

"What are they *arguing* about?" she said impatiently. "They've got a fair grievance, haven't they? I'd think they'd be unanimous about that."

"Oh, yes, they agree about the grievance. But what they can't decide is who is to be their spokesperson. Nobody wants the job."

"*Honestly!*" said Mum. "If you can't get a group of ghosts to behave sensibly, what hope is there for humans? I'd better go out, I suppose, and have a word with them."

So she did. She was there, sitting on the churchyard wall until about half-past midnight.

"The problem is," she said, coming in at last and making herself a cup of tea (I was watching the late late horror film), "the problem is they all want your great-aunt Millie for their spokesperson. And I'm quite sure Millie would be the last to begrudge her time and trouble – "

"So what's the matter?"

"Millie's grave is over in the north-east corner of the graveyard. Hasn't been disturbed."

I couldn't see any difficulty there . . .

And indeed, as things turned out, Great-aunt

Millie proved a real stand-by. Next evening her ghost (in MA cap and gown, accompanied by her horrible mangey old Airedale, Scrooge, who had frightened the life out of generations of students and postmen before he had a brush with a bull who finished him off) appeared at the Tudor Tango Country Club where Silas Inglejaw and his partner Jeremy Gussith were taking their wives out to dinner. Sat down at the same table with the Inglejaws, at a moment when Gussith and his wife were out on the dance floor. My friend Tilly Owens-Thomas who earns a bit of extra money by working as waitress was there; she said the smell of mothballs that surrounded Aunt Millie was quite something; you noticed it twenty feet away.

Of course the ghosts of an old University Chancellor and a savage mangey dog can make quite a sensation at a gala dance: Mrs Inglejaw let out a shriek like a burglar-alarm and fainted dead away, the rest of the customers panicked and made tracks for the car-park.

From then on, that was the way it was; wherever the partners went, Aunt Millie and mangey old Scrooge were sure to turn up. Whether it was in chapel on Sunday, or at Town Council meetings, in the office, their homes, in the doctor's waiting-room, on the motorway, or even on the beach at Newquay – Aunt Millie and her shaggy dog would be there. Smelling of mothballs.

"Put back those bones, Silas Inglejaw. Get those

bones back underground, Jeremy Gussith!" Aunt Millie would order, in a voice you could hear all up and down the beach. And Scrooge would howl. Awkward it was for them, really.

As a matter of fact, the town of Pen-y-Gent became quite famous; people used to come in coaches from all over the country, in hopes of hearing the ghostly command. Gussith and Inglejaw could have gone on TV; only, Millie and her dog were not cooperative and wouldn't appear if there were crews and cables about.

Two weeks of this treatment was enough. Inglejaw and Gussith had the bones replaced, as best they could, the tombstones set up straight, and the grave-yard tidied up, with brambles rooted out and new grass sown. Of course there was nothing they could do about the trees that had been cut, and Aunt Millie was very annoyed about this.

She appeared at a cricket match between Cardiff 2nd XI and Pen-y-Gent.

Just as Silas Inglejaw was bowling, she screeched at him: "What about those trees, you villain?" and the dog Scrooge fetched such a howl that Inglejaw's arm jerked and the ball went into the River Swilly.

That was the last straw for Inglejaw. He retired from the business, sold his share (it went for a song) and crept off to live in Malta. For a while after that Jeremy Gussith tried to carry on but his heart wasn't in it, because of the way Scrooge used to sit in his office and snarl at clients.

You see the trouble was that when Mum and my friend Tod's father and I dug up Aunt Millie we put her bones, and those of Scrooge, who was buried at her feet, like a Crusader's dog, in our greenhouse. And, during the re-burying, when we took them back, we discovered that Grandpa had put Scrooge's bones into his big green compost container and poured Barrington's Grade-A Compost Activator over them. So they had turned into compost and could not be re-buried. *Will Turn Even Old Rubber Tyres Into First-Class Compost*, it says on the side of the tin.

So mangey, bad-tempered old Scrooge is still around the town; and, as a result of that, though the other old ghosts went contentedly back into their graves, Aunt Millie isn't at all prepared to stay underground.

She turns up all the time, at meetings of the Bypass Committee, and the Twin-Town Selection Group, and the Parent-Teachers' Association. Jeremy Gussith, who at one time thought of standing for Mayor, has had to stand down. His nerves couldn't take seeing Aunt Millie scowling at him from under her shadowy mortarboard.

In fact there have been several suggestions that Aunt Millie should stand for Mayor herself.

Light Work

On a blistering, withering January day Uncle Avvie and Aunt Deena came to live in our tower block.

He isn't really an uncle but a second cousin twice removed of our dad who died when I was four.

"Twice removed. I wish it was twenty times removed," said Matt after a few days.

When I first saw Uncle Avvie, I thought he looked like a troll. His eyes were sunk so very far back in his head that they looked like bullets in gun-barrels; but they burned diamond-bright in their sockets. And his hands were as cold and hard as iron claws.

"So this is dear little Mattie and dear little Bessie. And the baby!" he said in a fruity chuckling voice.

"Matthew and Isabel and Charles," we corrected him, but he didn't listen. He was telling Mum how he and Aunt Deena had managed to get the top-floor flat, whipping it away from a widow with four children who had been at the top of the waiting-list.

"Ho, ho, it's just a case of knowing whose palm to grease, ho, ho, ho!" he said, laughing heartily. "That widow lady should have been a bit quicker off the mark."

I thought how horrible his cold bony hands would be when the palms were all covered with grease.

"Now, I hope you children are going to come and help us unpack," said Aunt Deena. Everything about Aunt Deena was thin: her voice, her hair, her feet, her face; she looked as if she had been tired from the day she was born.

"All right," we said, but not very willingly.

The lift wasn't working, as usual, so we followed Avvie and Deena up the grey stone steps in the grey stone stairwell to the seventh floor.

"Bit of a change from where we lived before, on the edge of the Dismal Swamp," Avvie said with his chuckle. "You ever hear of the Dismal Swamp, kiddiwinks?"

No, we said, we hadn't. So he told us it was a huge swamp in Virginia, America, full of alligators and bears and lynxes and rattlesnakes, and some other snakes called water-moccasins. Not a place I'd care to live myself, I thought, but very likely it suited Uncle Avvie.

He made us run about, unpacking boxes and cases, chests of china, and trunks full of clothes, shoving tables and cupboards into different positions, hanging pictures and mirrors on walls.

"Many hands make light work," he kept saying, rubbing his own claws together.

The pictures were very nasty, nearly all of them photos of the swamp, black and murky, full of dead-looking trees and trailing creepers.

Aunt Deena mostly just sat in a chair and looked tired.

After we'd worked like galley-slaves for nearly four hours, he gave us each a 10p piece. I nearly threw mine on the floor.

"What about that bag there?" asked Isabel, pointing to an old-fashioned upright leather bag with two handles and a clasp. It had a padlock on the clasp, and a red seal over the padlock. "Do you want that one unpacked?"

"No, sweetheart, thanks," said Uncle Avvie, laughing his head off. "That's my hand baggage, see? Nobody unpacks that one but me. And even I have to be very, *very* careful when I open it. Wouldn't you like to know why?"

Bell said that we'd be late for supper and we nipped away before he could tell us.

"I bet it was a horrible reason," said Bell as we ran down the stone stairs. "I think he's a creepy man. I bet he's foul to Aunt Deena."

"What happened to Mrs Fenwig?" I asked Mum when we were eating our chicken and chips.

"She fell off a balcony and broke her back and had to go into hospital," said Mum. "And her children had to go into care. It was quite a mystery why she fell; no one was anywhere near at the time but she said she thought she'd been pushed."

I thought that at least going into care would be better than living with Uncle Avvie. It was lucky for his children that he didn't have any.

His being there, up on the top floor, began to get us down; he dropped into our flat almost every day. He was much, much too close for comfort.

On his visits he told us more than we wanted to hear about the Dismal Swamp.

"If you don't know the right places to tread, you can sink right in, and that's the end of you. Plenty of people have walked into the Dismal Swamp and never come out again, never been seen – except maybe just their hands sticking out of the mud. Black as pitch, that mud is. At night time, you can hear the alligators coughing, and that's about all. Most people can't stand the swamp, it scares them to death, but it just suited me and Deena, didn't it, Deenie?"

Aunt Deena gave him her wan, nervous look.

"So why did you leave?" asked Mum, looking as if she wished they hadn't.

"Oh well, I'd finished my job there, dredging the canal." Uncle Avvie was some kind of engineer. "And I got what you might call a golden handshake." He grinned at us, showing a gold tooth. "So we thought we'd come back and see a bit of life. Shan't stay in this block very long – plan to find a decent house in a decent area – "

It was true that Uncle Avvie did go out a lot, to race-meetings and motor-shows, to clubs and cinemas and restaurants; whereas Aunt Deena never seemed to leave the building, just sat in the lounge all day long, looking at the gloomy photographs on the walls, picking at the fringe of the chair-arm cover.

Our old liver-and-white spaniel, Spindly (so called because she was so fat), didn't like Uncle Avvie at all. And he didn't like her. Every time he came through our front door she growled and howled and moaned and carried on; Mum had to shut her in the kitchen. Uncle Avvie laughed about it and said she probably thought he smelt of alligators. And he, if we went to his flat (which we didn't unless we couldn't help it) always asked if we'd washed our hands.

"Can't be too careful after touching a dog. Covered in germs, they are. So you just give those hands a good lathering with plenty of soap. Soap deferred maketh the heart sick. Where there's life there's soap," he said, laughing like a loon. Uncle Avvie was full of these quips and cracks.

One morning we found Spindly dead in her basket.

"Old age," said Mum sadly.

Bell said she was sure Uncle Avvie had crept in and strangled Spindly. "Look at the way her eyes bulge, and her tongue hangs out."

"Don't be silly," snapped Mum. "Spaniels' eyes always bulge. Anyway, how could Avvie get in the door? He hasn't a key." Thank goodness, said the look on her face.

"He could have climbed down the wall, like Dracula."

"He couldn't have got in the window."

The window is nailed so it won't open more than a couple of inches, because there are so many burglaries in our block.

Uncle Avvie popped in, later that day, and he laughed heartily when he heard the old dog had died.

"Well, well, we all come to it, all come to it, eh? So she'll never growl her head off at me again! How I'll miss the old tyke!" And he pulled a mock-sad face. "But what I came to ask you lot is, if you'll look in on old Deena this evening. I'm off to Blackpool – take a look at the snooker championships – shan't be home till tomorrow night. Deena's feeling a tiny bit low – got the female miseries, *you* know," he said, winking at Mum, "fancies herself worse than she is. If one of you lot would drop in every now and then, it'd cheer her up."

So of course we had to say we would, but after he had gone Bell said that probably just his being away would be as good as a tonic for Aunt Deena.

"You shouldn't say things like that," said Mum, but I think she privately agreed.

When I went up at tea-time, taking a slice of a

quiche Mum had made, it seemed to me that Aunt Deena was in a very queer state.

She hardly seemed to recognise me, she was walking fast about the room, flushed and restless, every now and then she'd double up and give a squawk, with what was clearly a shocking bad pain, and she was talking very wild.

"Oh, at night, at night!" she'd cry, "at night you hear all the dreadful noises from the swamp, and if you dare step outside you see all the withered hands reaching out of the slime, every single one of them holding a candle! But he put them out, Averon did; oh, he did, he did, he did!" And she burst into peals of frightening, hysterical laughter.

Well, I scooted down the stairs and got Mum, and Mum phoned the doctor, and he sent for an ambulance. But meanwhile one of us had to sit with Aunt Deena. Mum couldn't be there all the time, as she had to put Charlie to bed; so Bell and I stayed up in Aunt Deena's flat together.

By that time she didn't know either of us.

She was talking all along, more and more crazy stuff about hands reaching out from the swamp.

"With the big sugar nippers, he cut off their flippers!" she screeched. "And now they have to work for him – like slaves. All hands on deck, he says. Oh, heaven help us, what will ever happen if they get out?"

Then the ambulance came and carried her off.

Mum got fussed while they were putting Deena on the stretcher because, she said, the hospital would want to know where they could get in touch with Uncle Avvie, and Deena was past telling them that, and we didn't know, except that he was in Blackpool.

"Maybe the address is by the phone – I suppose he's at a hotel?" I suggested.

But no address was there, and Mum had to go with Aunt Deena in the ambulance.

"Look – here's her keys – be good children and have a hunt in the desk, see if you can find any address written down, and I'll phone you from the hospital. And then you lock up and bring the keys down to our place."

She went off, following the attendants with the stretcher.

Bell went home to keep an eye on Charlie, I took the bunch of keys and unlocked the desk, which was in the room Avvie called his "den".

All the papers inside were very neat, and I couldn't find a Blackpool address anywhere. I looked in all the other likely places – behind the clock, on the dressing-table. Most likely, I thought, Avvie didn't leave any address when he went off; most likely he preferred to feel he was out of reach.

Then my eye fell on the locked bag. It was made of thick heavy leather, about two feet in length and a foot high – what used to be called a Gladstone bag. The handles at the top were held together by a metal clasp, and that was fastened by a padlock. And the padlock was covered by a red wax seal with what looked like a geometrical diagram stamped on it.

I can't say what came over me. I didn't really think it probable that Avvie would have left his address in the bag. The only words that found their way into my head whispered: "Would one of those keys fit that padlock?"

Naturally I had to break the wax seal to uncover the keyhole. As I did that, I heard a queer stifled sound – like the noise a whistling kettle makes if you run hot water over the lid when it is empty. The noise made my fingers tingle.

Then I tried various keys. And the smallest one fitted.

So I undid the padlock, and took it off, and raised the hasp that held the two sloping sides of the bag together.

Really I was quite nervous, expecting I don't know what – that something would jump out at me, a monkey, maybe, or one of those moccasin snakes. But nothing did. In the bag was what I at first took to be a pile of old leather gloves, white and black and dark-brown and limp – a whole mass of them, thirty or forty perhaps. Who in the world would keep forty leather gloves locked up in a Gladstone bag?

Then – perhaps my hand shook, holding the bag – I thought the pile seemed to heave and wriggle, like live fish that have just been netted. I slammed the two edges of the bag together, jammed down the catch, hooked back the padlock . . . but then I couldn't get it to fasten. Maybe a bit of sealing wax had got into the wards. No way in the world would it lock. So, in the end, I had to leave it, with the hasp just hooked over.

I locked the door of the flat – you can be sure of *that* – ran down the stairs, locked our door, and said nothing to Bell.

By and by the phone rang.

"That's probably Mum," said Bell. "I'll take it."

She picked up the phone. Then her face changed. "Oh – hullo Uncle Avvie," she said awkwardly. "Yes – yes I do – no, that's why you got no answer on your phone. Aunt Deena had to go into hospital. Yes, Mum got the doctor and went with her. No, I'm afraid I don't know which hospital. Mum said she would ring, but she hasn't yet. So we don't yet know what's the matter. About an hour ago."

She listened for a bit, pressing her lips tight together, then put down the receiver. "He sounded really annoyed," she said. "As if Aunt Deena had no right to be ill! But he said he'd try to come back on the midnight train."

When Mum arrived home she looked more cheerful, though tired. "It's only Deena's appendix," she said. "Ought to be all right in a few days. Lucky it didn't happen when they were off in that Dismal

66

Swamp. Lord knows who'd have looked after her there."

My spine crept a bit, thinking of the bagful of leather gloves upstairs.

Bell told Mum about Uncle Avvie's call and how he expected to be back after midnight.

"Oh dear," Mum said, "I suppose I ought to sit up for him."

I suggested that I should have a nap now, and then she could wake me at eleven and I'd sit up while she got a bit of sleep.

That was what we did.

About one-thirty in the morning I heard a taxi pull up in Egland Road, outside the front entrance of our block. Looking out of our kitchen window I saw the cab come out from under the portico and drive away.

I went to the flat front door and opened it, ready to intercept Uncle Avvie as he came up the stairs. (As usual, the lift wasn't working.) As I opened the door I heard a pitter-patter, very quick and quiet, going along the landing outside – like a lot of small creatures, rats, maybe.

We do have rats in our block, sometimes. They climb up the sides of the garbage disposal pulley.

I pushed the front door to, prickling with sweat; then got a hold on myself, opened it again, and went out on to the landing. Looking down over the banister rail I heard somebody begin to come up the stairs, walking slowly.

"Is that you, Uncle Avvie?" I called in a quiet voice.

I heard Mum stir inside the flat – she'd been sleeping in a chair – and she came out, buttoning her candle-wick housecoat.

"Who d'you think it is?" I heard Avvie's voice call back irritably. Then he seemed to suck his breath in. Next we heard a really shattering scream – it sounded as if his soul was being torn backwards out of his body – and a loud smacking thud. He'd gone over the banisters, fallen clean down from the fifth to the ground floor.

When the police came and took him away, they said he hadn't died from the fall, but from suffocation. Could you believe it? They said his nostrils were stuffed full of soap, and there was soap in his throat too. They never did find an explanation for that. Luckily no one could say Mum or I had done it since old Mrs Crabtree, who never goes to sleep, had peeped out of her door and seen him go by, and she saw him throw himself over the rail, waving his hands, she said, as if he were trying to push something away.

Aunt Deena got better and came out of hospital, and she's living in Southend now. We helped pack up her furniture and stuff. The Gladstone bag was empty, and she couldn't or wouldn't say what Avvie had kept in it.

My friend Habib-ullah, who helps his father run

the fruit-stall on the corner of Egland Road, told me
that yesterday evening he distinctly saw a wet whitish
hand climb up the corner stanchion of the stall – fast,
like a squirrel – snatch a tangerine, and then scurry
off again, down the dark street.

An Ill Wind

y cousin Cherry McCleod came from Canada to stay with us for a couple of school terms. Her name is really Irina Natasha, but everybody calls her Cherry. Her elder brother had died in an accident, and Cherry herself had been badly ill with jaundice, and Aunt Tanya thought it would be good for Cherry to go away and meet some unknown cousins and have a change of scene. So she came. She was six months younger than I am, but seemed older, perhaps because of having travelled all that distance by herself, or the shock of losing her brother – they had been very close, Aunt Tanya wrote. The McLeods live way out in the middle of Canada where it's all forest for hundreds and hundreds of miles. Aunt Tanya, of course, originally came from Russia, from the steppes; so I suppose that huge Canadian land-scape seemed quite homelike to her.

Cherry found England's smallness quite surprising at first – all the neat little fields and crisscrossing roads. But she seemed to like it well enough. Forests can be a bit frightening, she said, when you remember it may be possible to go on through them for days and days without any chance of seeing a house or meeting another person. And there are practically no paths or tracks.

I had expected that Cherry would find Netherstoke Common and Bayford Head, which are our nearest bits of wild land, pretty tame by comparison. But she seemed content with them. The autumn term wouldn't begin for a couple of weeks yet, so we went about on bikes, to the beach if it was fine, and picked plums at Ridgwells' fruit farm, and did the shopping for Mum, who was busy bottling and making jam. Cherry and I got on well; she is gentle and friendly, fond of cats and small children; she likes dressmaking and singing in choirs.

One day I'd stayed at home getting on with my holiday assignment of reading *Macbeth* (a horrible play) when Cherry came back from the Wondermart where she had been shopping for Mum looking bothered and rather sick.

"What's up, love?" asked Mother when Cherry gave her the jam-pot labels and pectin she'd gone for. "You're as pale as if you'd seen a ghost."

I noticed Father, who had just come in and was taking off his garden boots, give Mum a sharp look and shake his head. And her hand flew to her mouth as if she'd remembered something, just too late.

But Cherry said, "No, I didn't see a ghost. But something rather nasty happened in the supermarket. Well – no – not nasty, that's silly. Just awkward. It was nothing really."

"Tell us what it was," said Dad. "Telling always helps get rid of it."

Cherry said, "I was standing in the line at the check-out counter with my basket of stuff. There were three or four people ahead of me, just standing and waiting. Directly in front of me was an elderly lady, and in front of *her* another old lady, with white hair, wearing a plaid suit. She hadn't a metal basket; she was holding two things, a wrapped cake and a big carton of double cream. And I saw her open her patent-leather bag-purse and quietly tuck the pot of cream inside – it was rather a tight fit.

"Then, looking up, she caught my eye fixed on her. I wasn't frowning at her, or anything like that. I guess I was just looking rather blank, wondering if she planned to carry the cream home in the bag. It seemed a crazy thing to do, suppose it leaked out and got all over her money! That was all that was in my mind. I hadn't thought about stealing – she was well dressed, she didn't *look* like the kind of old girl who'd go in for shoplifting. But then she gave me such an awful look – really scarey . . . I can't describe it! As if her eyes were drills and they were boring right through me. And she whipped the cream out of her purse, and went on, and paid for it at the desk, and walked out of the store. That's all – but somehow it upset me."

"You don't know who she was?"

"I'd not seen her before," said Cherry. "But the checkout girl seemed to know her, I heard her say 'Hullo, Mrs Wildeve.'"

Father and Mother exchanged looks.

I said, "Oh, gosh, Mrs Wildeve!"

"What's special about her?" Cherry asked.

"Dad calls her Aunt Boreas. He made up a rhyme about her:

> Don't make Aunt Boreas
> Furious
> Or she'll whip up a force ten breeze
> And blow you off the Pyrenees."

Too late I saw the urgent face Mum was making at me.

"That's just a lot of nonsense," she said quickly. "Mrs Wildeve used to be head of the Primary School. She's retired now. She's just a perfectly ordinary old lady."

"Anyway," I said, "she doesn't know who *you* are, Cherry. Or where you live."

"Why?" Cherry asked. "What difference would it make if she did?"

"Ennis, will you go and get me one of the big bags of preserving sugar from the pantry," Mum said, and when I went to get it she came after me into the pantry, and hissed in my ear, "Will you kindly shut up about Mrs Wildeve? We don't want to make Cherry more nervous than she is – "

"What *do* you mean?" I said, rather puzzled. "Is she nervous?"

"Oh, my heavens." Mother snatched the sugar from me. "This is what comes of not *telling* things. I told your father it would be better if you knew – "

"Knew what, for goodness' sake?"

"I can't tell you now. Later. But lay off talking about Mrs Wildeve, will you?"

"If you say so." I was still bewildered.

But of course the harm was done.

My friend Hero Jones came round to play table-tennis. She knows everybody for miles around and all the tales about them.

"Old Wildeve?" she said. "If you've got in *her* bad books, you'd better look out for squalls, and I mean *squalls!*"

"What do you mean?" said Cherry.

"There was Freddie Spencer, who ran over Mrs Wildeve's cat on his motorbike. A week later he was riding along that road, Swithin's Edge, that goes up to Bayford Head, and the wind blew him, bike and all, clean over the cliff. There were several fellows behind and in front of him – it was a rally – but they didn't get blown off, only him."

"I don't see that proves anything," said Cherry.

But I noticed she was a little pale.

"That's not all. There was Mr Pendennis the vicar. She said he'd got her sacked from the primary school."

"I thought she retired?"

"She was asked to resign because she and the other teachers couldn't agree. A couple of months later, Mr Pendennis was cutting a branch off his cherry tree and a gust of wind blew over the ladder. Broke his neck."

"People get very careless with ladders," I said, scowling horribly at Hero. "I heard of somebody who sawed off the branch his ladder was leaning *on*."

But Hero went on, ignoring the faces I was making at her. "Then there was Gordon Gregory. He and Mrs Wildeve had a row about some trees at the bottom of his paddock, where it meets her garden. Ash trees. She said they were her trees, he said no, and he cut them down."

"What happened to him?" asked Cherry with fearful interest.

"Went on holiday in the Pyrenees. Climbing with a guide. They get terrible storms down there, wind and thunder and lightning. He got blown into a crevasse – his body was never found."

"Excuse me," said Cherry. "I don't feel very well."

"Did I say something wrong?" demanded Hero Jones when Cherry, white as a sheet, had dashed upstairs.

Mother blew in like a hurricane.

"Idiots! With your stupid chatter! Why didn't you *warn* Hero, Ennis?"

"What about?" I asked. "You've not said yet."

So then Mother told us.

"It was about Lewis. The way he died."

Lewis was Cherry's elder brother.

"How did he die?"

"Dick and Tanya didn't want it mentioned – they said it upset Cherry so much. Apparently Lewis read some tale about a great beast that lives in the wilderness – the Canadian forest. He got fascinated by it. And he wanted to go and look for it. He went off, back-packing, with a couple of friends – a big storm blew up and they got separated. Two of them made their way back to the camp – but Lewis said this creature always came out in a gale, that was the time to find it. It had some name connected with wind, I forget now – "

"What happened?"

"Lewis was never found. They had search parties out for months – but there wasn't a trace – and that upset Cherry *terribly*. Not knowing what had happened to him."

"Oh, *poor* Cherry."

I had known that Cherry and her brother were very close, but not that there was some mystery about his death. She never talked about him. Never mentioned him.

"So the *last* thing we want," said Ma emphatically, "the very *last* thing – is for a lot of nonsense and talk about Mrs Wildeve and – and *wind*. And people dying unexpectedly, or disappearing – "

"Well I'm sorry," I said, and I was, very, "but it would have been much better if you'd warned us about all this before."

"Oh, I know – " Mum rubbed her brow distractedly. "Aunt Tanya said not to talk about it to *anybody* – but now I see how wrong she was – "

Cherry came down later, pale but composed, and the name of Mrs Wildeve was not mentioned again. But I could see in the next few days that Cherry wasn't sleeping well, she looked wan, her eyes had dark rings under them, and some mornings she admitted she'd had bad dreams – she didn't say what about.

School began, and Cherry fitted in there well enough; she was ahead of us in some subjects, behind in others. She made friends and got into the junior hockey XI.

Then, one afternoon, Cherry and I were riding home from school on the bus when I noticed an old girl, about three seats behind us, giving Cherry a very sharp steady stare.

It was Mrs Wildeve.

I didn't say anything to Cherry, who hadn't noticed her, but it struck me that it would not be a good thing for Mrs W. to find out that Cherry lived with us, so

I said, "They've got that ballet film *Cat Among the Pigeons* on at the Plaza Quad. Why don't we go on into town and see it?"

I thought that way, if the old girl followed us, she'd lose us in the shopping centre.

But that was no use. Cherry said, "No, I'm tired, and I've an awful lot of French to do. Let's see it some other night. I'd rather go straight home."

So we got off the bus, and I noticed that Mrs Wildeve did too, though it wasn't her stop. Her little house is up on St Swithin's Edge.

I still didn't say anything, because I didn't want to fuss Cherry. I said, "D'you mind if we go the long way round the block? I want to buy a pair of shoelaces at Penny's."

"I'll go straight home," said Cherry, but I said, "Oh, come along. I'll buy you a Sundew bar."

So she came, rather unwillingly; but that was no use either. Mrs Wildeve was waiting, fifty yards off, on the other side of the street, when we came out of Penny's shop, and she moved along after us, never looking at us directly, but keeping in view.

Now I was definitely alarmed.

Cherry still hadn't seen her. But she shivered and said, "It's turned awfully cold, all of a sudden, hasn't it? I'll sure be glad to get indoors."

When we went into the house I saw the old girl, still far away down the street, standing under a lamp post, steadily watching us.

I didn't like it one bit.

I remembered some of the other things Hero Jones had said about Mrs Wildeve: "She's supposed to wear an old bit of rag round her neck, with three knots in it. If she unties one of the knots, there'll be a high wind. Two knots, there's a storm. And if she undoes all three knots, that brings a whole hurricane."

"Just hark at the blessed wind!" said Ma when we were eating tea. "I've staked my dahlias, but they're never going to stand up to this. And all the apples will be down before they are ripe."

"What's got into the doors?" said Father. "None of them will stay shut."

It was true. The doors were creaking and shifting on their hinges, swinging and groaning and banging. On a sudden wild gust, the front door flew wide open, and thereafter refused to stay closed unless it was double-locked.

"It's like an invisible army trying to get into the house," muttered Father, who is not usually given to flights of fancy.

Cherry was very quiet all through tea, and kept shifting her chair. "Wherever I sit, there seems to be a draught," she said, and shivered again.

"Not coming down with a cold, are you?" asked Mum. "Better put on a thicker sweater. Remember, English houses aren't so warm as Canadian ones."

All that evening the wind howled and howled.

"It's like a human voice!" exclaimed Mother, who

was trying to watch a TV quiz programme. "Sounds as if somebody's outside, calling and calling. I can hardly hear what the people say."

Cherry and I took our work up to her bedroom, which has thick curtains and double-glazed windows, but we could hear the wind whipping and moaning outside, the rain tap-tap-tapping on the panes.

"It *is* like a voice," muttered Cherry. "Like what Lewis used to say about the voice of the Wendigo."

It was the first time she had mentioned her brother.

"The Wendigo? What's that?"

"It's a great creature that lives out in the forest. Lewis read about it in a book." Cherry glanced towards the windows, and went on, "It can travel through the air, terribly fast, in huge leaps. And it leaves huge footprints behind."

"Like Abominable Snowmen," I said, shivering. "Perhaps they are the same?"

Cherry huddled in her chair, hugging her arms round herself, as if she were unbearably cold. "I wish I were at home!" she said miserably. "I want to go back to Canada. There, at least, I shan't be so far from Lewis – wherever he is. I'm going to write and say I don't want to stay here any longer."

"Don't do that! Talk to Mum first," I said, terribly bothered. "Wait till tomorrow. You might feel differently then. After all, you'd have to book a flight – and tell the school. You can't just leave, like that. Wait and talk to Mum."

"I'll talk to her," said Cherry, "but I'm going to write and ask if I can come home, right *now*."

She scribbled an air letter very fast, and said she was going out to post it.

"I'll come too," I said. "Wouldn't mind a walk."

It wasn't true. I didn't in the least want to go out into the black, howling night.

We walked along to post her letter in the post-office box, which has the earliest collection. Coming back, we were about to cross the busy road in front of the post office, stepping between a line of parked cars, when a driver slowed, just beside Cherry, and rolled down his car window.

"Be a kind girl and post this for me, will you?" he said, "to save me having to find a parking-space – " and he held out an envelope.

"Of course," said Cherry, and stepped back on to the pavement with his letter. As she posted it there was the most tremendous crash – and all the traffic in the street shot forward. A huge tree at the end of the block had blown down, with its entire length along the road, smashing two traffic islands. Amazingly, no one was hurt, though the whole street was in chaos. If the traffic hadn't accelerated just in time, two cars at least would have been crushed. And if Cherry hadn't turned back to post the man's letter, she would have been in the middle of the road when the tree fell.

We had to walk right along to Station Road, to get across there.

"I c-c-can't believe it!" Cherry kept saying, through chattering teeth. "I w-wish I could find that man again, to thank him. He seemed so kind – I suppose he's miles away by now."

"What did he look like? I didn't get a glimpse of him."

"White beard – blue eyes – like a r-rather nice uncle."

I had a queer thought. But I kept it to myself.

"Who was his letter addressed to?" I said.

"It's funny you should ask that."

"Why?"

"I just glanced at it, as I put it in the box. And the name stuck in my mind – I'm pretty sure it was addressed to *Everyman, Esq.*"

"No initial?"

"I'm not sure. I remembered it because – " her voice trembled, "that's what I used to call Lewis sometimes, in fun. 'Mr Everyman.' Oh, Ennis – I *do* wish I was at home. It isn't that I don't like it here – "

"I know. Come along," I said, catching her cold hand. "Let's run. It's freezing! You've written your letter – you can't do more."

We scooted up the street, and my hands shook as I shoved the key into the keyhole because, about six feet away from the front door, I'd almost thought there was a person standing outside it, waiting. But of course it was only the shadow of the Virginia creeper.

"C-can I come and sleep in your room tonight?" Cherry asked. "I don't like the sound the wind makes in mine."

"Of course you can!"

So she came and slept with me and we both tried to pretend that nothing was the matter. But I heard Cherry crying in her sleep, and in the morning she told me she'd had horrible dreams.

"About the Wendigo. I heard it crying *Lew-is*! *Lew-is*! And then it called my name – *Irina*! *Irina*! And I *knew* that, sooner or later, I'd have to go with it."

Mother was horrified when I told her about this.

"She can't go back to Canada yet! I know Tanya wouldn't want it. She'd only get ill again."

A week went by, cold, fidgety weather. I didn't see Mrs Wildeve, but, almost every time I came back to the house, I *thought* I saw her, out of the corner of my eye. As I walked along the road I'd have a fleeting impression of a skinny old girl, with white blowing hair, waiting in the shadow at the side of the door. Then, when I reached the house, I'd see that it was just an illusion, a trick of light and dark.

I didn't ask Cherry if she thought she saw anything; quite honestly, I didn't dare.

There were gales all that week. A chimney-pot blew off the cake factory beside our playing-field and hit Cherry on the back of her head. She had slight

concussion; the school doctor said it wasn't bad enough for hospital, but he brought her home in his car and she had to stay at home for several days. Privately, Mum told me she was glad of a chance to keep Cherry under wraps and cosset her a bit. And it seemed to me an excellent thing that she should be kept out of the way of displaced chimney-pots and falling trees.

"Dad," I said next day – I was helping him sweep up fallen leaves in the front garden – "what do you really think about Mrs Wildeve?"

He stopped and rubbed his head.

Then he said, "The universe is full of forces, isn't it? Heat – X-rays – radio waves – electricity – things we don't understand, but make use of. I think some people are more tuned in to these forces than others. I read about a man who had to be sacked from a factory because he fused all the generators every time he walked past them. And some people are healers – if they put their hands on you they can warm you, or drive away a headache. Mr Pendennis could do that, I heard – the vicar who died."

"So you think Mrs Wildeve – ?"

"Oh, I don't know, I don't know!"

"Why should she have such a horrible nature – stealing, quarrelling, bearing grudges?"

"Only humans show kindness," said Father. "Nature isn't kind. Human kindness is something that takes generations of good behaviour to produce. If a person is more in harmony with a natural force – such as wind – than to politeness or charity – "

He left his sentence unfinished.

"But where does poor Cherry come into this?" I said, dumping an armful of leaves into the wheelbarrow. "Why, just because of something she saw – such a trifle – "

"Cherry may be extra vulnerable. Because of her brother, because of what happened to him. Perhaps because of her heredity."

Vaguely, I thought I could see what he was getting at.

"Cherry's in our care. We have to look after her," he said. "Dammit, is that the phone ringing? Can you run in – my hands are covered in mud."

We could hear the sound through the front hall window. I raced inside – it might be Aunt Tanya.

But the voice was a male one. It asked, "Can I speak to Irina?"

Rather astonished – "She's having a nap at the moment," I said, which was true. "Can I take a message?"

"I wanted to ask her to come out with me."

"She's ill at present," I said, even more astonished, because Cherry had not acquired any boy friends at school. "You'd better wait and call again in a week or so – what name shall I tell her?"

The line became very faint, and crackled. I thought

I heard the name "Gregory . . . " Then it went quite dead.

Rather shakily, I replaced the receiver.

"It wasn't your aunt Tanya?" asked Father when I went back to the garden.

"No," I said. "No, it wasn't. It was someone for Cherry . . . "

I didn't tell Cherry about the call.

But next day when I got home from school, Mum said, "A very queer boy came to the house, inquiring for Cherry. Wanted her to come out with him, if you please! I said certainly not, she was in bed, ill. I was really glad to have a good excuse to say no – I didn't like the look of him at all!"

"What was he like?" I asked with a fluttering heart.

"Untidy," said Mum. "Leather jacket and trousers – all wet and tattered. I know it's a rainy day – but he could have put a comb through his hair – "

"Did he give his name?"

"Fred – Ted – some name like that. Impertinence, I call it! She probably hardly knows him."

"Did you tell her?"

Mum shook her head. "I'll wait till she's better. As I said – I didn't fancy his looks."

Cherry took quite a while to get back on her feet. Dr Marston said he couldn't really understand it. "There's nothing physically wrong. But, if she's been under strain back at home – if she's still distressed about her brother – that could account for it."

A few days later, Dad and Mum had to go to Exminster for a big legal meeting about the bypass that planners want to build round our town. By this time Cherry was coming downstairs, convalescent, but not yet allowed out of doors.

"You two will be all right, won't you?" said Mother. "There's plenty of cold chicken in the larder and we shan't be late – the meeting ought to end at half-past nine or so, we should be back by eleven."

"We'll be fine," I said stoutly, concealing some private doubts.

I got home from school at five, and Mother and Dad went off in the car at half-past. Not long after they had left, it began to rain, and the wind got up, slapping the trees about, slamming people's front gates, bowling over empty dustbins. Then the rain changed to snow, and the temperature shot down.

Presently, as Cherry and I were watching *Vet Your Life*, the phone rang.

I raced for it.

"Oh – Mum – hullo! Anything wrong?"

"No, love – but we're not going to be able to get back tonight. There's just been a police announcement that half a mile of the coast road fell into the sea. So we have to stay the night here with the Windleshams. Will you and Cherry be all right?"

"Of course," I lied.

"Mind you check that all the doors and windows are locked."

"Of course," I said again, looking through the hall window at the blizzard of thick snow which was blowing sideways. "It's a very good thing you aren't going to drive back. The weather's awful."

Dad came on the line to say check the boiler and turn up the heat. "Goodnight, chickabiddy. Sleep tight! We'll be back in the morning by the inland road. And this is the number where we are." He gave it, then rang off.

I put the receiver down, feeling rather hollow. And, looking past the phone, out of the window, through the blizzard, felt the hollowness turn to pure terror.

For there, with her white webby hair and her grey webby skirt blowing in the wind, came Mrs Wildeve; right up to the front door she walked, and I heard the zing of the front door bell. I tapped on the window to attract her attention, and shook my head vigorously. Her eyes met mine, she gave me a long, cold stare, then the bell went again, a long, thrilling peal.

"Someone at the door!" called Cherry, who was in the kitchen with the TV. "Shall I go?"

"No, no, it's all right . . . "

I shook my head again, even more emphatically, at Mrs Wildeve, and made go-away gestures. She glared at me. I remembered Cherry saying, "Her eyes bored into me like drills." They were exactly like that. In another minute I'm going to have to open the door, I thought. I'm going to have to.

I tried to make a picture in my mind of some harmless everyday object – any image to put some kind of barrier between me and the cold unchained anger, the pure malevolence and wildness that waited there outside the door.

Curiously enough, what came first into my mind was a kind of mental film sequence of posting a letter. Putting the square white thing in the letterbox; hearing it fall, in the certainty that, because of the address written on it, because of the postage stamp, that square of white will be taken off, by unknown hands, in a mail-van, a train, a plane, a ferry, a sleigh, maybe even a rickshaw or a camel, perhaps to the farthest possible point, the extreme opposite corner of the globe. Reliable human hands will get that letter to its destination. *That promise will be kept.*

I thought of the square white envelope. Mr Everyman. Then I looked out of the window again. Mrs Wildeve was gone.

And, thank goodness, the blizzard was slackening off. A glint of moonshine appeared through the hurrying clouds.

I went back to Cherry. She looked very tense. "Who was it at the front door?" she asked.

I told a lie. I said it was somebody collecting for the lifeboat fund. Before she could ask why they would do it in such weather, I gave her Mum and Dad's message about not getting back tonight. She was disturbed by the news, I could see.

"We'll be all alone? I wish we weren't. Do you know what I thought, when the bell rang? I thought, Suppose that is Lewis, out there. His ghost, you know; come for me."

"What utter rubbish!" I scolded. "For heaven's sake, Lewis was your *brother*. He loved you! He wouldn't want to take you away – out of life – "

"Why not?" Cherry asked in a remote voice. "How do we know what he would want?"

"Oh, nuts!" I snapped. "You shouldn't think of such things. I'm going to make some hot chocolate, and then we'd better go to bed."

I put the milk on in a saucepan, then remembered Dad had said to check the boiler, which is in the cellar. I went down while the milk was heating. Then, on my way back up the cellar stair, I heard the phone ring. Also the doorbell again.

Oh heavens! I thought.

First I raced to the kitchen to grab the milk, which was just about to froth all over the stove. Then to the phone, still relentlessly ringing.

"Ennis? Is that you? It's Aunt Tanya here. Listen – *they found Lewis's body*. Will you tell Cherry that? It was curled up – very peaceful – in a little cave – as if he had died in his sleep. Will you tell her? Or put her on the line?"

"I'll put her on," I said, and then suddenly the meaning of the icy draught that was curling round my ankles hit me.

The front door stood open.

"*Cherry!*" I called loudly. "It's your mother!" But there was no answer. My voice echoed emptily in the empty house.

"Aunt T-Tanya?" I said into the phone, my teeth chattering. "Cherry d-doesn't seem to be about. Maybe she went out to post a letter. I'll get her to call you. She'll be – she'll be so happy and relieved – "

Then, with hands that could scarcely hold it, I put back the receiver, dragged on a windcheater, and raced out of the house.

Outside, the snow had stopped; the moon shone. There was an inch of snow on the path. Cherry's footprints were perfectly plain, from the door to the garden gate, along the road.

But what made my heart like a lump of ice in my chest was the fact that, beside Cherry's footprints, there were others. Not very frequent – one print to every twenty of hers, as if her companion were taking huge, unbelievably huge strides. And the print wasn't the shape of a human foot, either.

I followed, along the road, along the path by the football field, up the side of Bayford Head, which stood like a great snowy triangle against the dark sky. The wind hissed in my ears, and froze the tears on my face, and the surf roared and thrashed down below at the foot of the cliff. I could see great clouds of white spray burst up over the cliff-edge from time to time.

Every now and then I called, "Cherry! Where are you? Cherry, come back!" but my voice was carried away on the wind.

The path goes about sixteen feet from the verge of the cliff, no closer, because bits of cliff edge are always falling off. There's no guard rail.

When I got to the top I could see nobody.

I'm too late, I thought. She's gone.

Then, far along, right on the brink, I saw a small, crouched shape. There was a saddle-shaped dip, where a bit of cliff-top was getting ready to fall. She was huddled right into that.

"Cherry! What are you doing there?"

I almost tiptoed towards her, over the snowy grass. Then knelt, and crawled, and stretched out a careful hand. A single jerk, almost anything, I felt, might unloose that corner of crumbly ground, make it slide down into the boiling sea below.

Cherry stared at me, rather puzzled, like someone waking from deep sleep.

"Ennis? Hullo? What are you doing here?" She echoed my words.

"Speak for yourself!"

The tips of my fingers just touched hers. I edged a couple of inches nearer, caught hold of her wrist, and gently drew her towards me. I didn't want to frighten or startle her.

"Come along," I said. "It's far too cold to stay here. Come along home, Cherry."

And, very slowly, she moved towards me.

In a few minutes we were walking steadily back the way we had come, obliterating with our footprints the ones that had led in the other direction.

"I believe I must have fallen asleep," Cherry said in a dreamy, puzzled voice. "I was talking to someone – a man – just before you came. *Was* it a dream? I suppose it must have been. He told me that the letter had got to Lewis, that Lewis was safe . . . "

"*Who* was telling you this?"

"I'd know him again," she said with certainty. "I half recognised him. Yes – now I know. He was the man in the car."

"The man in the car."

"Who asked me to post the letter."

"But why did you run out of the house?" I asked, as we turned the corner into our road. The wind was still pushing us from side to side, but it seemed less cold now, or we were warm from hurrying. I forgot to notice if anybody was lurking by the front door.

"Why did I go out? Because I heard Lewis calling me," she said matter-of-factly.

I slammed the door behind us, double-locked it, and put the key in my pocket.

While I reheated the milk and made chocolate, I told Cherry about her mother's phone call. She cried a bit; but gently, not hysterically. Then we went to bed, and slept right through till ten o'clock next morning, when Dad and Mum woke us by ringing and banging at the front door.

In the local paper it said that two cottages had been thrown into the sea by a cliff subsidence brought on in last night's severe gale. One cottage had been standing empty; the owner of the other, Mrs Virginia Wildeve, was missing, feared drowned.

I hope she stays missing, I thought.

Cherry was glancing over my shoulder at the inside page.

"That's him!" she said. "That's the man who talked to me. The man in the car. I knew I'd know him again."

Memorial Service, said the headline. "There will be a memorial service on the 23rd in St Christopher's Church for the Reverend Matthew Pendennis who died in a tragic accident two months ago . . . "

"He came and held my hand," said Cherry with total conviction. "He said it wasn't my turn yet, there were things waiting for me to do. And he thanked me for posting the letter. He said that a message will always get to its destination if you really, really mean it to . . . "

Bindweed

It was when I was cleaning the dining-room windows that I first saw Aunt Lily, or thought I did. After she was dead, I mean. You know how, when you stand outside a window and rub off the white smears of window-clean fluid, by the time the glass is really shining and clear it acts as a mirror. You can see the sky behind you, quite dazzling; trees and buildings and the ground go dark, like a photographic transparency. It was our garden that I could see re-flected, with the big walnut tree and the stretch of lawn, and a bit of the valley beyond, and a cloudy white sky; then, across this scene, carrying a white parasol, strolled our Aunt Lily, who had been dead for a year.

I was so startled that I dropped the container of Busy-BMart window cleaner and made a big pink splash all over the nasturtiums.

"Alan! Now look what you've done!" scolded Mum, passing by. It was a Saturday morning. I was earning five pounds to go bowling in the afternoon with Sandy Swithinbank. Cleaning all the downstairs windows, inside and out, double-glazing included, is a hard-earned five pounds, I can tell you. Specially with Aunt Lily thrown in.

I picked up the plastic container and, when Mum had gone on her way, peered warily back into the spotless glass of the window I had just polished. The trees hung idle and dark, the grass was bright green, with my brother Claud mowing it over in the far left-hand corner; everything was just as it should be, except that Claud would have to hurry if he was to get the grass cut before the rain came; there was a big mass of thunder-cloud piling up behind St Ebb's steeple.

No sign of Aunt Lily.

It was simply imagination, I thought with huge relief. Optical illusion. A trick of the eye. Something close at hand – a floating dandelion puff, maybe – had taken the shape of Aunt Lily's white parasol (which I knew Mum had gladly hurried off to Oxfam a week after the funeral – all Aunt Lily's belongings had flown from the house like meteorites the minute she quit it herself; nobody had wished to be reminded of her one minute longer than necessary). The notion of Aunt Lily's parasol had conjured up the old monster herself. You hear a zoom and see a vapour-trail and you think you see the plane itself. Something like that.

I thought no more of the matter, finished the windows, just before the downpour, collected my five quid from Mum and spent the afternoon bowling with Sandy, bringing him back afterwards for supper, which was Indian takeaway.

The thunderstorm, which had muttered and circled around, and gone away, and come back, all afternoon, was now well into its stride. In fact Sandy and I got properly soaked, cycling back from the bowling-rink at Portsbourne; he came up to my bedroom to dry off and borrow a pair of jeans and a T-shirt.

While we were drying our hair a tremendous flash of violet-coloured lightning made all the lights go out for a moment and illuminated the garden outside my window – the creeper and walnut tree shone a sinister livid green.

"That's funny," I heard Sandy say, as we waited for the shattering peal of thunder that followed.

"What's funny?"

He was glancing towards the window and I didn't catch his reply, which was drowned in the rumpus; it sounded as if giant babies were hurling about mammoth building blocks in the sky above us.

He didn't answer, so I repeated my question when the row had died down and the lights had come on, rather flickeringly.

"Oh, nothing. Just a crazy notion I had."

He was rather silent even after we went downstairs and started on the potato chahkee and mutton dopiaza and onion bhajis.

By and by Claud came in, irritated because the Allington golfcourse had been submerged under a flash flood and the tournament he was due to play in had been put off. My brother Claud has won a whole lot of golf trophies, silver ones. They stand on brackets all over the house. I suppose somebody has to play golf – plenty of people apparently *do* – but I've never yet met a golf player that I liked. My brother Claud is no exception. Even good-natured Sandy agrees that he is a pill.

Now he began putting us down because of our vulgar habits.

"Only erks ride pushbikes and go bowling."

"Erk yourself," I said huffily. "Golf is just a snobs' game."

At that moment a searing glare of lightning cut out all the lights once more.

"Oh dear," said Mum as we sat in the semi-darkness. "How long will they be off this time, I wonder? I want to watch *Catch 'Em Alive* at nine."

As the thunder let off yet another salvo, close at hand, something clanged in the house.

"What in the world was that?" cried Mum. "Sounded as if a coal scuttle fell down."

"Coal scuttles don't fall down, Mother dear," said Claud patiently. "Coal scuttles are down already."

Claud is always snubbing Mother and Dad in the same way that he used to put down Aunt Lily every time she opened her mouth. He excels at the art of humiliating people; I expect he will end up working for the DHSS. He is also quite a hand at practical jokes – scattering a teaspoonful of sand in your muesli while you aren't looking, or putting on the speed of the record player from 33 to 45 just before Mum plays her favourite LP. The history teacher at Markham School, Mr Jevons, suffered from a severe breakdown and had to take a term's leave of absence when he was Claud's form master. Of course that was a couple of years ago. Claud is in the Sixth now, and acts as if he were the Lord Chief Archangel; but his nature is still the same.

The lights came on again and Dad stumped in, knocking the rain off his hair.

"Blasted weather!" he said. "Just when I wanted to get to work on the bindweed. If I don't get it dug up this weekend, the whole garden will be covered with the stuff. I've never known such a year for it."

Bindweed is that creeping stuff, wild convolvulus; it has rather pretty pink-and-white flowers, but it's real murder in the garden; climbs over everything, and the roots go down to Australia. They are fragile thin white brittle things: pull at them and they all break off. You have to dig down, sometimes about four feet, ever so carefully, to get them all out; and you never *do* get them all out. Dad really hates the stuff. "Lilies," the old country men in the village call bindweed, "they botherin' lilies."

"Why don't you use weedkiller?" said Mum as she always does.

"Because of the birds," said Dad, as *he* always does.

Claud threw up his eyes, for patience.

"One of your golf cups fell down, Claud," said Dad, helping himself to mutton and catching Claud's expression. "It's rolling around in the front hall."

"*That's* what the clang was," said Mum.

Claud bustled out, looking annoyed, and we heard him set the cup back on its bracket. Then we heard him give an odd kind of grunt, before he reappeared in the kitchen, slightly paler than usual.

"What's up?" said Mum. "You sickening for something?"

But he shook his head and said he was going upstairs to sort out his stamps. That's another thing he does: corresponds with fellow stamp-collectors all over the world.

Three minutes later he was back down, looking very mad indeed.

"Who's been in my room, messing about with my stamps?"

He glared at me and Sandy.

We said truthfully that we hadn't been near his room, and Mum confirmed this.

"Well, somebody has, and my stamps are all *wet* — some of them ruined, very likely."

"You probably left your window open." Mum wasn't very sympathetic. "Now, you lot, hurry up and finish, I want to get the dishes done."

As we dried the cups, she said, "Just think – it's the anniversary of Aunt Lily's death. Remember all the plates she used to break, by putting them in the rack at an angle, so they fell through? And how cross she used to get, and say it was our fault for having a plate-rack that was too big."

We began happily remembering other things about Aunt Lily: how her eyes used to dart round the table, furtively, to make sure no other member of the family had a bigger helping than hers; how she used to fuss if her pension cheque didn't arrive on the first of the month, by the first post, and would get Mum to phone the building society; how her bedroom table and window sill were completely covered with little bottles and jars that she referred to as "the remedies". How her money, pinned inside her corsets was "the wealth". How she gave off a potent reek of liquorice allsorts and how, after her death, we found a huge tin cashbox, stuffed with them, under her bed.

Aunt Lily, Father's elder brother's wife, had nagged Uncle Tom to death (or so Father always says). He fell out of his bedroom window, or jumped out. Then Aunt Lily, having got through Uncle Tom's savings, was obliged to come and live with us.

Claud hated her worst, but we all found her a trial. "I do want to pull my weight in the household," she was always saying. "I do want to be one of the family."

But – bar drying a plate or two, and breaking many more – she never actually did anything useful about the place, housework or shopping or assistance with cooking or cleaning. She appeared, promptly enough, for meals, and bundled off to her room pretty smartly after them again, saying that she was very tired, and had to lie down.

If it was fine, she'd sit in the garden with her old white parasol. Indeed, all summer long she wore white clothes, droopy old things that looked as if they had come from some jumble sale. "She thinks she's Miss Havisham," snarled Claud. If Mum had hung out laundry on the line, Aunt Lily would fiddle about with it, turning things round; "I'm helping your mother," she'd say with a saintly air. She might pull off a few rose-heads, not cutting down to the main stalk, where it would be some use, but just tweaking off the dead flower, so someone would have to go round after her, doing it over again; or she'd snap off the leaves of a few weeds, not rooting them up, just breaking the stalks.

"*Don't* do that, Lily," Father would say, time and again. "It only makes them sprout thicker, don't you see? They have to be dug up with a *fork*. I'll fetch you one from the tool-shed if you like."

"Oh, no, thank you, Edward dear. That would be too much for my poor heart. I have to be careful. But

I do like to do my little bit; if I pull off the bindweed flowers, that will stop them from seeding. And it makes the garden look just a little tidier."

"They don't *seed*, they spread by *rooting*," Father ground through his teeth, but she never listened.

Claud took no stock in the tales about Aunt Lily's poor heart. "I bet it's just indigestion because of the way she gobbles her food."

Claud had a running battle with Aunt Lily about toast. It was his job to make the toast for breakfast, and he always put Lily's piece at the bottom of the pile, to get soft and flabby. If it was scrambled egg, he'd pour the scrambled-egg liquid all over her toast beforehand, to make it thoroughly damp.

"*I don't like soggy toast!*" she'd hiss at him furiously through her dentures, chomping away on the sodden stuff, and Claud would put on his most innocent air, and answer every time, "Oh, don't you, Aunt Lily? But I specially made it that way for you. I thought you liked your toast to be as soft as possible. I really thought so!"

She'd glare daggers at him but, because Claud is fair and handsome, and looks very like what Father's brother Tom did when *he* was young, she could never bring herself to be unduly nasty to him. Whereas with the rest of us she could be really sharp.

"Don't you speak to me like that, young man! You just wait till you are sixty! Then you won't think it such a joke to laugh at a poor old lady!"

Having her in the house was like permanent wet weather. Very depressing. But we all supposed we were stuck with her for years and years; despite the talk about her poor heart she seemed in superb general health and never caught so much as a cold.

Then, one evening, just a year ago, there was a power failure. (Later we heard that the cause was Sandy Swithinbank's father who, with Sandy's help, had been lopping a rotten branch off the huge, half-dead wild cherry that grows at the bottom of his garden. The branch fell on the power line and cut off the current from half the village for nine hours.)

So there we were, groping about the house with candles and oil lamps.

Claud, who was still sore from a set-to he'd had with Aunt Lily about Sunday TV programmes – *Songs of Worship* conflicted with *Comanche Trail* and, of course, being an old lady and our guest, she had to have her choice – saw in this situation a chance to get a bit of his own back.

He tiptoed up astern of Aunt Lily on the upstairs landing, as she was cautiously feeling her way from the bathroom to her bedroom door, and suddenly grabbed her from behind, saying, "Boo!"

She let out the most extraordinary gasping wail, like a punctured balloon. "Ah-h-h-h-h-h!" I heard it through my bedroom door, which was open, and doubled up laughing – it was an incredibly funny sound. Still makes me laugh to remember.

Then she sank to the floor. "Like a stick of boiled rhubarb," as Claud said.

"Oh – Aunt Lily! Is that *you?*" he cried, in pretended dismay. "I'm so very sorry! I thought it was Alan. Here, take my arm."

All kindness and solicitude, he hoisted her up and led her to her bed, where he helped her lie down and covered her with one of her old camphor-smelling shawls. Then, gasping with suppressed laughter, he came to our room.

"Did you hear her? *That'll* teach the old so-and-so to grumble because Dad has six mushrooms on his plate and she has only five!"

For once, I and my brother saw eye to eye. Both of us thought that Aunt Lily had richly deserved her fright.

After a while, the electricity came on again and we all resumed what we had been doing before; no one gave Aunt Lily another thought until Father, going up to bed at midnight, noticed that her bedroom light was still shining under her door, so tapped and looked in to see if she was all right, and found her cold and dead in her bed.

It seemed that the talk about her poor old heart had not been a lot of eyewash after all.

She was cremated, by the wish expressed in her will (which left £162, all her worldly wealth, to Father) and the ashes were scattered in our garden, also by her wish.

"I *suppose* they will be good for the ground," Father said rather gloomily, as the fine, surprisingly heavy white stuff lay about on the lily-of-the-valley leaves under the big walnut tree. Unfortunately it was a dry month, and the ashes continued to lie there day after day, embarrassingly reminding us of our deceased aunt, and the embarrassing way she had died.

Nobody blamed Claud; no one spoke of it; but he went about very subdued, not at all his usual self, for quite a number of weeks. At last, of course, he recovered, and was worse than before. Perhaps the practical benefits of what he had done suddenly struck him: Aunt Lily removed, he got back the use of his own room (he'd had to share with me while she lived in the house), so, in fact, his evil deed had really paid off.

Not – of course – that he had meant to *kill* the old girl.

Anyway, after a month it rained, her ashes washed down into the soil, and we all forgot about her; apart from my recent imagined glimpse reflected in the window, and Mother's musing remark over the drying-up: "Just think, it's the anniversary of Aunt Lily's death."

"Funny you should have remembered Aunt Lily," observed Dad, wiping the last glass and putting it on the shelf with the others. "Just now, in the front hall, when there was that big flash of lightning, I could have sworn I saw her, in that old white dress of hers, standing outside the glass panes of the front door."

"Must have been the white lightning," Mother suggested.

"I expect so. Hark at that blessed rain! The bindweed will be growing an inch an hour," Dad grumbled. "It's absolutely smothering the lilies under the walnut tree. And now it's started up in the rosebed alongside the house. The rain had better stop by tomorrow, that's all I can say."

The third step in our staircase tends to crack like a rifle-shot when somebody steps on it. We heard that noise after Father spoke. Sandy, who was sitting opposite the open door into the front hall, suddenly drew in a sharp breath, as if he had toothache.

"Is that you, Claud?" called Mother. "If you're going up, could you fetch my knitting bag? It's on the bookcase in my bedroom."

There was no answer.

"It couldn't have been Claud," I said. "Claud is upstairs already."

"That's funny."

Mother went out into the hall, carrying a lamp.

"Claud?" she called. Still there was no answer, so she ran up and fetched her own knitting. Claud could be deaf as a post to other people's requests when he chose, and he generally did choose.

"The sudden humidity is probably making the floorboards warp," Dad said when Mother came back. "But surely you can't see to knit in this light?"

"I don't have to see when I knit. Can you put me on a record, Alan?"

"No power," I reminded her.

"Oh, bother! Nor there is."

There came a slight lull in the rain, and Sandy said he thought he'd go home. He was rather quiet and glum, and I couldn't blame him. The house felt strangely cheerless, and not only because of the dim yellow lamplight. Something murky and hostile seemed to be close around us in the sultry dense night.

"I'll bring your jeans back tomorrow – or the next day," Sandy said, glancing warily about the garden as he mounted his bike and switched on the light. "So long – see you – " and he was off down the path like a *Tour de France* contestant. And I was back inside at the same speed because, idiotically, improbably, through the drips of rain from the sodden trees, I could have sworn that I heard Aunt Lily's thin, complaining whiny voice call, "Claud! Claud! Come here, Claud, I want you."

I hurled myself inside, slamming and locking the front door, and, thank goodness, at that moment, all the lights came on. I heard Mother's and Father's voices from the kitchen, raised in cheerful relief. The dazzling light made my previous thoughts seem even crazier. Just the same, something prompted me to go upstairs. The third step was silent this time – it always is, if somebody else has just stepped on it. I went to Claud's door and banged on it.

"Hey, Claud? Are you in there? Can I – can I borrow your Latin dictionary? I left mine at school."

Claud didn't answer, so I opened the bedroom door. The first thing I noticed was his window, flung wide open, with a pool of rainwater on the sill.

Then I saw the soles of his feet.

They were *outside* the window.

Upside down.

"Dad – *Dad!*" I yelled – hysterically I expect – and dashed across the room to the window. The dark outside seemed even more opaque because of the lights having just come on. I could dimly see that Claud appeared to be hanging head down, just below the window; but not what held him there.

Luckily at that moment Father arrived, could hardly believe what he saw, but took command in a practical way.

"Grab his ankles – hold them – don't let him go! – while I fetch a ladder."

So I clung for dear life on to Claud's ankles while, in about three minutes flat, Father got the ladder from the garage and leant it up against the wall by Claud's window. Between us – Mother was in the room too, by now, helping me to hold Claud – we got him undone from a thick tangle of coiled and twisted plant tendrils that was wrapped all over him. Judging by the mass of stuff, you would have thought he'd hung there for days, for weeks. I got out my penknife and was cutting through the stems; Mother sawed away

with a kitchen carver. Then she ran down to the garden and helped Dad lower my brother gingerly to the ground, among all the leaves and entwined stalks and squashed white flowers.

The plant had grown up the side of the house in a huge matted mass, like ivy.

"It's *bindweed*," said Father, in a tone of total disbelief.

"But poor, poor Claud!" Mother was crying. "Is he alive?"

"His heart's still beating," said Father, feeling it.

We carried him indoors and, while we waited for the doctor's arrival, gave Claud artificial respiration, and pulled armfuls of bindweed loose from him. His face was dark and congested, but he was still breathing – just.

Another five minutes in that position, said the doctor, and he wouldn't have been – and how, in heaven's name, had he *got* into that position?

Needless to say, the doctor wouldn't accept any of our accounts of what had happened. Or, at least, he wouldn't have, he said, if he hadn't been acquainted with old Aunt Lily; but he could believe anything, he admitted, of that old Tartar. And he gave Claud a massive injection, to put him to sleep for twelve hours, and recommended that somebody should sleep in his room with him.

"Just in case the bindweed climbs in through the window."

But it didn't. It seemed that Aunt Lily had shot her bolt.

Next day Father went out with a set face and a big can of Slaughterweed and painted the poison over every bindweed stem in the garden. Very soon they began to shrivel up and turn black.

"The birds must take their chance," said Father.

Claud remained thin, white, and silent for weeks after. Months. He said he couldn't remember a single thing that had happened, except he had a notion he'd heard Aunt Lily grumbling about something.

By and by he went off to university, and now seems quite a changed character; but, personally, I doubt if the change will last.

I asked Sandy, when he brought back my jeans, why he had left our house so fast.

"Because I saw the old girl," he said. "From the kitchen. I thought I must be going off my chump. I saw her come in the front door and go up the stairs."

"She must have gone into Claud's room and tipped him out of the window. Maybe that was what she did to her old man."

"Maybe he gave her soggy toast too," said Sandy.

Amberland

ust a year ago I made myself stop dreaming about Amberland. I stopped thinking about it too. Put it right out of my head and planned for it to stay out. You can do that if you really set yourself to it. No more walking on those silvery beaches or picking fruit in the sweet-scented woods. All that had to go. I won't say I didn't miss it.

Well, I have to start further back.

Amberland belonged to me in the first place. It was mine, I found it. Can't say how. I just did, and knew it was mine. At that time it wasn't called Amberland. I just thought about it as *There*, or *The Happy Island*.

It was Dolph, my brother, who said it ought to have a proper name.

I'd never meant to tell Dolph about it, let him in on it. He was a pain, a whiny, moody, runny-nosed little creep, four years younger than me. Mam was always on at me to play with him, keep him amused, take him with me when I went out with the other kids. "The bairn," she called him – as if there was no other bairn in the whole world. Of course I didn't want him with me. Who wants to be saddled with someone that much younger? And Dolph was a puny little object, quite a few folk thought he was daft, because his head was so big, much too big for the rest of his size, and his arms and legs thin as sticks – and then his feet turned out sideways like a duck's; he walked with this funny wobble. "Rachitic," the doctor at the clinic said. Whatever that means. The kids down the block called him "Duckfoot" or "Ducky" and lots of them thought he really did have birds' feet. Well – to tell the truth – that was mainly my fault, for I'd told my friend Dougal that Dolph's feet were yellow, with claws, and that was why he always had to wear two pairs of socks, and in no time the tale had got all over the neighbourhood. Kids used to run after Dolph and yell, "Take yer socks off, Shorty! Let's see yer tippy-toes!" and after that he wouldn't go out on his own. That was why Mam always made me take him with me when I went on an errand for her, otherwise he'd never have left our flat, or got any fresh air.

It was one time, coming back with kail and taties from the market, carrying heavy loads, and him whining and grizzling all the way home, that, just to put a stop to his grumbles, I first told him about the Place.

"Where is it? Can I go there?" he wanted to know at once.

"Only if you dream about it," I told him.

"What like of a place is it, Randy?"

"Och," I said, "it's just beautiful. There's beaches that's all soft, white sand, miles and miles. And the sea's so warm. And then there's woods with oranges and coconuts growing, and friendly monkeys that'll let ye play with them – and birds – "

"And shops? Is there shops?"

"No shops," I said. "Everything you want is just growing on trees."

At first, he was a bit disappointed about the shops. But soon he began to have ideas of his own about the place. He'd come to breakfast with his eyes huge and bright.

"Randy! I dreamed about the Place!" he'd whisper when Mam had her back turned, frying the bread and tomaties. And he'd give me a nod, important-like, as if there was lots to tell.

I was a bit irked, I won't deny, at the way he'd just walked in and, as it were, grabbed himself a share of my Place without me telling him he could. And at first I couldn't believe he'd really dreamed about it; I reckoned he was just inventing the dreams to impress me. But, by and by, he got so wild enthusiastic about it, and there was such a lot of stuff he tumbled out, mountains and torrents and waterfalls and all, that I did begin to wonder. Because, if he *didn't* dream it, where the morran was it all *coming* from?

Sometimes I got really mad at him and used to shut him up.

"It's my Place. You've no right to talk about it!"

Then he'd wail and whimper and carry on to Mam: "Make Randy say I can go there, *make* him!"

And Mam, without the least notion what we were talking about, busy and bothered as always, washing a great pile of table-linen and napkins for the Caledonian Hotel, what we called the Caley, would bawl at me: "Randy! Why can't ye play friendly with the wean and let him do what he wants? Ye're the elder, you should have the more sense. Now, hang out this line of cloths for me and then, if ye can't get along indoors, take the bairn for an airing, and shift yourselves out of my way."

I'd have to hoist and haul the heavy line of dripping cloths across the alley, by the pulley, while folk walked past, four storeys down below, never noticing, and little Dolph, curled up on the old broken-backed armchair, gave me a grin of triumph.

Then, while Mam began on a new tub of washing, I had to take the little beggar down the street and put up with yells of "Ducky! Ducky! Take yer socks off!"

Many times I was tempted to run down the road and leave him, for he could only hobble slowly, but I knew if I did Mam would give me a terrible tanning.

When I was with him he didn't mind the hoots and catcalls.

"Och! They're no more noise than the birds make, in our Place," he'd say, shuffling by my side. "All those eagles and penguins and – and albatrosses – d'ye mind what a deal of racket they make?"

Albatrosses! I thought. Where in the name of goodness did he get those from?

When he was four Dolph learned himself to read. Not that there were many books at our place. Dad hadn't ever been a great reader. He was a foundry worker, and died in a fire. But our granda, Mam's dad, had been a schoolmaster in some little back-of-beyond place, and there were a two-three books of his at the bottom of the closet – rubbed old things with the covers coming away and loose pages. One of them was full of poems. And, plugging his way through this one, as he began to, day after day, Dolph found all kinds of things. He'd grab me, with his eyes blazing.

"Hey! Listen to this. It's just our Place!

'He hangs in shades the Orange bright
Like golden lamps in a green Night.'

Did you ever hear anything liker? And then – wait – listen:

'And makes the hollow Seas that roar
Proclaim the ambergris on shore – '

that's those little yellow bits that lie about on the tidemark. And then:

> 'He cast (of which we rather boast)
> The Gospels Pearl upon our coast.'

Isn't that the spit and likeness of our island, Randy? It must be the same! Our sandy beaches are all scattered oo'er in pearls and shiny yellow beads, just like yon in the poem. It's our place, ye can see that for sure! I'm going to call it Amberland."

You're going to call it Amberland, I thought. Who found it first? Whose place *is* it?

Just the same, I fell into the habit of using that name with Dolph. He talked about it so much that we'd both be dreaming of it, night after night.

"There's a cave up there in the white cliff," he'd say, munching on his bannock. "I wonder what's inside there? Treasure, most like! I'll get up there tonight and have a look."

"You!" I'd scoff. "You couldn't climb up to that cave – it's away too high! You'd never get up there. I'll go, sometime, and take a look. Maybe it's a dragon's cave. You're too weak and puny for climbing."

"On our island I'm not weak and puny," he'd say tearfully. "I'm not, I'm not lame there. I'm as big as you – and can run as fast. Anyway – there's no dragons on our island."

"Well, not a dragon, but something nasty that might jump out on ye."

Dolph sometimes got so upset that Mam would give me a skelp on the lug.

"Randy! Give over teasing the bairn!"

"All right, all right! Have it your own way. Go in the cave! What do *I* care?"

Soon as that was settled he'd simmer down and tell me the other things he'd seen – the upside-down star trees growing along the top of the cliff, the deep waters under the island where huge monsters, turned to rock, stood supporting the whole mass of it on their backs, like fire-dogs.

"Tell ye what – there's a University!" he said one day proudly.

"A *university*? You daftie! How *can* there be?"

For there were no other folk at all on the island, only Dolph and me.

"What use in the world would that be? Who wants it?"

"*I* don't know," Dolph said. "But it's there, for I saw it last night."

"What for should there be a university?"

"It's up in the forest at the far, hilly end of the island. A big, towering old place – like a palace – hundreds and hundreds of years old, all built of brick, old red brick, with trees and creepers grown up a' round it till ye can hardly see it – and a terrible great wooden door, old thick wood that's half eaten away, wi' a lion's head knocker. It's called Brazenose."

"Brazenose? Why?"

"I don't know why," said Dolph.

"It's not needed," I said. "I don't want it on my island."

I was really sore about it, specially as Dolph was so obstinate.

"There's a deal of books in there, in the old library, and I'm gaun to read them a'."

"Suit yourself," I snapped, and I went out to play with the boys on the block. I'd had enough of Dolph.

But, just the same, the notion of the huge old crumbling brick building among the tangled trees stuck in my mind, and try as I would I couldn't get rid of it. And it began to spoil the place for me. I loved the island the way it was before, with just the trees and the fruits, melons, figs, pineapples and pomegranates – and the friendly birds that came with gifts for us – and the gentle sea, endlessly breaking on those miles of silvery sand spangled with pearls and glistening lumps of amber. No footprints anywhere, not a one . . .

"*Hey, Randy!*" shouted my friend Dougal across the street. "Want to join the Gulls?"

The Gulls were a famous gang and it was a big honour to be asked. Of course I said yes.

After I joined the Gulls, I didn't stop at home any more, I was always out in the street with the gang. And when Dolph told me some tale about Amberland,

I'd tell him, "Och, dinna fidget me with that childish stuff now. I've no time for all that." It wasn't the truth, for I still dreamed about the island two nights out of three, wandering in its woods or along its coast. But now, each time I went there, I found myself shadowed by the thought of that great old brick building hidden away in the northern woods. Who wanted a university? Was that truly what it was? Or if not, what? Who was inside there? Had my brother been in there? Doing what? Studying? Studying *what*?

Then there was the cave in the cliff: a dark oblong hole, cut among the white stones. Every now and then, as I passed along the beach below, something seemed to stir in there. A person? A creature? Who would stay in such a place?

"Something nasty that might jump out on ye," I had said to Dolph. Now I wished I hadn't.

My bonny island was turning into a haunted place. There were sounds that I could not quite hear, and movements that I was not quick enough to catch.

Now that I hung around with the Gulls gang there was no one to take Dolph out. Mam was too busy always with her washing. Times he got very low-spirited.

"Why can't *I* join that gang too?"

"You? They'd not have you! You're too ailing and peaky and wee!"

It was true, the last few weeks, his head seemed to have grown bigger, his arms and legs thinner.

"Well, ask 'em – do!" he persisted. "Ask 'em if I canna join?"

Of course I knew they'd never have him.

"They'd no' take a young 'un with birds' feet," I teased him.

"You know that's no' true!" he roared out furiously.

And, day after day, he was on at me about it, until Mam said, "Oh, for pity's sake, Randy, ask yer friends if the wean canna join their club. It'd only be a token membership, like."

"Oh, very well," I grumbled. But of course I didn't. I knew they'd only laugh, and I didn't want them to remember that I was the brother of Dolph the duck-foot. So when he asked me, all breathless, "Did ye tell them about me, Randy? Did ye?" I said, "You can't join unless you do the initiation ceremony."

"Did *you* do that?" he said eagerly.

"Of course! Everybody does."

"What did ye have to do?"

"I had to walk on my hands across the tracks on Mearns railway bridge," I invented.

"Well – I could do that! I'm none so bad at walking on my hands."

"It has to be different for each person."

"What would mine be, then?"

"To go hand-over-hand across the alley on the washing lines," I said, for I knew he was awful terrified of heights. I thought that would shut him up once for all.

He did turn white as one of Mam's napkins. But he said, "Well, I'll do it. I'll do it now, while Mam's out taking the clean laundry. Open the windy."

"*No!*" I said. "No, stop! It's daft! Don't do it. Forget I said it."

But once he got an idea in his head, you couldn't turn Dolph.

"I want to join the Gulls," he said. "Then I'd be gaun out wi' you and we could talk about Amberland the way we used. Open the windy."

He couldn't reach the top catch, it was too high.

When I opened it, he took a terrible gulp of air. He had turned even whiter – a sort of greenish colour. Then he knelt on the sill, took a hold on the washing lines – there were three of them, greasy sooty old things – and shut his eyes. Then he took and shoved himself off the ledge and was hanging there with his face turned up, eyes still closed. Then he began to shift himself along, sideways, dangling and swinging about. His little yellow hands were like birds' claws as they clutched the greasy old rope. I couldn't stand to watch, so I shut my eyes too, but after a little time – I don't know, maybe four minutes? – I heard a wail, so I opened them again, quick. I don't think the wail was from Dolph. I saw him start to fall, one of the ropes had broken and he'd lost his grip on the others.

Then he went down.

After Dolph's funeral – the Friendly Society helped Mam with the undertaker's fee – we moved to another building. Mam couldn't stand that one any more. We were on the other side of town, so I lost touch with the Gulls. I found another gang called the Braesiders and joined that instead. And I made myself stop thinking about Amberland. Blocked it off. Pulled down a shutter over the whole place. Didn't go near it, didn't dream about it.

Until last night, which was the anniversary of Dolph's death. Mam had been talking and crying and rocking and moaning, I suppose that set me off. And I dreamed I was back there.

As in the old days, the woods were full of jewelled trees, with oranges burning bright, purple figs, honey-coloured melons, tasselled pineapples. Far off in the distance, among a dark cedar cover, was that University, a huge silent place full of books that nobody could read. Or that I couldn't read, at least.

I turned my back and walked the other way, down to the beach. Smooth, smooth gleaming white sand, sprinkled with pearls and yellow stones. Not a footprint anywhere, except the prints of birds. And there, on my left, were the cliffs, like a high wall of white

rock, with the upside-down star trees burning in a fringe along the top.

And there was the cave in the cliff, a dark hole with something – somebody? – stirring inside it.

I didn't want to go any closer to it, but somehow I had to.

The shape inside, biggish and sluggish and white, stirred itself, and stretched out a foot, two feet. Yellow feet with claws, not birds' feet, not human. Somewhere halfway between.

It was Dolph, my brother, but he had changed.

I managed to wake up out of that dream, so fast that I felt I'd left a bit of me behind there, gulping and cowering on the cold beach.

What'll I do now?

I daren't go to sleep again, ever in this world. Not for the rest of my living days. But how can a person get along without sleep?